Trouble for Paddy Joe

Paddy Joe and his Alsatian, Storm, had lived with the Colonel and Tomkin ever since his grandmother's death. Now they were to go to an island off the west coast of Scotland for a holiday. It was a superb place for a holiday: beaches, woods, caves and plenty of wild life. And Paddy Joe and Storm found plenty of places to explore – until the day Storm disappeared.

They searched and searched, and no trace of the dog could be found. He had utterly vanished. But Paddy Joe was determined not to give up. . . .

Other books by Joyce Stranger

JASON
VET ON CALL
DOUBLE TROUBLE
VET RIDING HIGH
NO MORE HORSES
D.I.A.L. VET
THE FOX AT DRUMMERS' DARKNESS
THE CURSE OF SEAL VALLEY
PADDY JOE

All published by Carousel Books

Trouble for Paddy Joe
Joyce Stranger

A Carousel Book
Transworld Publishers Ltd

To Leslie

TROUBLE FOR PADDY JOE

A CAROUSEL BOOK 0 552 52243 0

First published in Great Britain by William Collins Ltd.

PRINTING HISTORY
William Collins Ltd edition published 1973
Carousel edition published 1983

Carousel Books are published by
Transworld Publishers Ltd.,
Century House, 61–63 Uxbridge Road,
Ealing, London W5 5SA

Made and printed in Great Britain by
Hunt Barnard Printing Ltd., Aylesbury, Bucks.

1

'Paddy Joe!' The shout fragmented the silence.

Tomkin was angry, and Paddy Joe shifted his position.

He was hidden in the branches of the apple tree, outside his bedroom window; his Alsatian, Storm, lying on the ground beneath. They had escaped from duty. Paddy Joe was tired of duty. He was tired of schoolwork and homework and jobs that had to be done before bedtime. He wanted to sit and dream in the dusky garden and be young again without responsibility. Growing up, the Colonel said, meant responsibility. It meant sharing in the life of your home, and not being a passenger. It meant looking after your own dog, and not expecting other people to exercise him, feed him, groom him, train him.

He had been lazy about the dog's training, and Storm had run off that morning and not come home when Tomkin called. The dog had been waiting for Paddy Joe at four o'clock outside the school gates. The conductor refused to allow them on the bus, as he was afraid of the handsome Alsatian, and Paddy Joe and Storm had to walk five miles. They were very late indeed. When the bus had arrived without them Tomkin had been worried. Worry sharpened his tongue and he was furious by the time boy and dog reached home.

Paddy Joe was an orphan. His parents died in an

accident when he was only one year old, and he lived with his grandmother until she too died. Paddy Joe overheard Mr Throstle, Grandee's lawyer, tell the vicar that Paddy Joe would have to go into a boys' home and that Storm, his dog, would have to be put to sleep. Paddy Joe ran away.

He stayed away for two weeks, knowing that the Colonel, who was on holiday, and who was Grandee's best friend, would look after Storm. In fact, when the Colonel came home, he became Paddy Joe's guardian, and bought his grandmother's house, as his own was too small. Tomkin, who had been the Colonel's batman during the war and now looked after the old man, looked after Paddy Joe too. Martha, who had worked for Grandee, had her own two rooms in the big old-fashioned house, and kept to them. She was very frail and nearly eighty, and, said the Colonel, had earned a rest.

Life with the Colonel was very different. Grandee and Martha had done everything for Paddy Joe, and he had always been banned from the kitchen when there was work to do. Now he was expected to help, to fetch eggs from the farm, to cook Storm's meat and give the dog his meal, to wash the plate and to remember to fill the Alsatian's water bowl.

Today he had gone to school without remembering the dog's water and the dinner plate stayed dirty and Storm ran off because Paddy Joe had spent too much time playing with the dog and none at all on his training sessions. Dogs have short memories, Tomkin said, over and over again. You can't ever relax. You must go on with their lessons for all of their lives, and he must come when he's called, Paddy Joe.

And the dog refused to come back to Tomkin.

Grandee would have been angry, but her anger would have melted when Paddy Joe apologised.

8

Tomkin was still angry, with a cold anger that was worse than reproaches. Paddy Joe climbed down from the tree, reluctance slowing every movement. He was tall for his age, his skin tanned and his brown eyes vivid. He did not want to go indoors.

But indoors had to be faced, and when he went into the kitchen he found Storm's dirty plate standing by itself in the centre of the newly scrubbed kitchen table. Tomkin was reading the paper. He did not even lift his head when Paddy Joe came into the room, and the man's small thin figure was tense. The grin was missing from his face. The room was too silent, the ticking clock as noisy a rebuke as Tomkin's stillness. Paddy Joe took the plate to the sink, and began to scrub it. Yesterday's meat was stuck hard, and it was far from easy to clean. It would have been much better to do it as soon as the dog finished eating but there had been other things to think about.

Paddy Joe wanted to see the new American satellite shoot across the sky; he wanted to look for the hedgehog that bustled through the garden each evening and watch it drink its bread and milk. He wanted to walk in the woods when it was night and fear was a thickening in the throat and almost a hidden pleasure, because the Colonel had forbidden him to wander alone in the darkness. Both he and Tomkin were afraid Paddy Joe might run off again. Paddy Joe was too impulsive, too easily hurt, too ready to take offence. And Grandee's death was too recent. And Paddy Joe never thought about danger. The world was a dangerous place, and he must remember.

'Don't be too hard on the boy,' Paddy Joe heard the Colonel say.

'He has to learn. The old lady spoilt him. He's much too young for his age,' Tomkin answered. 'It's not easy, growing up in the world today. The sooner he knows what's what, the easier it will be when he's grown.'

The Colonel walked away without answering. Paddy Joe sighed. Life was composed of difficulties. As soon as one problem was solved another came along and each seemed bigger than the last. It was not easy to settle down and remember everything.

Paddy Joe suspected his own memory was as short as his dog's. Storm was watching him now, sharpset for food. His ears were cocked and his eyes bright, and though he sat patiently, he inched forward eagerly, and saliva dripped from the corner of his mouth. The clock struck nine. The dog was always fed at seven. Tomkin looked across at Paddy Joe and said nothing, and Storm, so hungry that he forgot his manners, stood up and barked, impatient to be fed. Guilt needled again. Paddy Joe dried the plate and went to the store for the tin of dog food. He went back to the kitchen. The tin opener was missing.

It was not hanging on the hook. It was not in the drawer, nor on the table. Tomkin was watching, his eyes bleak, and Paddy Joe knew he had put the beastly thing down somewhere the day before, and forgotten where. Storm barked again.

'Think on, Paddy Joe,' Tomkin said, the anger still in his voice. 'Where did you go yesterday with that dog?'

Paddy Joe had fed the Alsatian in the empty stable. Tomkin had been busy in the kitchen and had sent boy and dog outside. Paddy Joe went out to the stable, his dog following him. The tin opener lay on the rickety old bench that stood by the door. He picked up the opener and went indoors, and when Tomkin looked at him with an exasperated tightlipped mouth, Paddy Joe flushed, and began, hastily, to open the tin.

He was in too much of a hurry. The opener slipped, and next moment Paddy Joe was looking in dismay at

10

the blood that stained the newly cleaned table.

'For the love of heaven,' Tomkin said, angrily. He took the tin from Paddy Joe and finished opening it, and put the food down for the dog, every movement quick and neat and deft. 'Go and wash that cut. Don't just stand there bleeding, boy!'

Nothing ever went right.

Paddy Joe held his finger under the tap and watched the water flow red. The cut hurt, and tears pricked behind his eyes and his throat ached. Everyone was against him. It wasn't fair. He wished Grandee were alive again. He wished that Martha would come out of her room and comfort him as she had when he was small.

'There, Lambie, Lambie,' she used to say. 'There, let Martha do it for you.'

Now no one did anything for him. Now he lived in a masculine household and everything was different. All the big soft arm-chairs had been replaced by deep leather chairs, comfortable enough, but smelling of tobacco, so that rooms once fragrant with Grandee's flowery perfume seemed totally alien. The cupboard that had housed Grandee's needlework and his games now housed three guns and was always locked. The guns were forbidden, never to be touched and punishment would be dire should he disobey. Paddy Joe knew how to shoot, and he knew the rules about guns, and those at least he understood, and would never dream of breaking. But there were others that seemed less important.

The little room where Martha used to sit at night was full of angling equipment. Rods and reels and fishing line; weights and hooks and flies; paternosters and traces and tins with meticulous neat little labels on them; books about fish and fishing. Paddy Joe liked fishing, and Tomkin had taught him a good deal, even when

Grandee was alive, but he was not yet used to the changes in the house. Only his own room was the same, was a familiar retreat, along with the apple tree, where he loved to sit, hidden in the branches, and watch the speeding trains.

Tomkin brought antiseptic cream and plaster and covered the cut. Storm finished his food and went into the garden. Paddy Joe wanted to follow, but this time he would wash the plate immediately and then he would not forget. He picked it up and rinsed it under the tap and for the first time Tomkin smiled.

'You'll do, boy,' he said, and squeezed Paddy Joe's shoulder, and suddenly the world was bright again. Storm returned to the kitchen and settled to sleep in the corner, and Paddy Joe sat in the wicker chair on the other side of the hearthrug. A woodfire burned in the grate. The evening was cold, although the weather had been fine and warm with a blue sky brighter than many a summer day. It was late September.

'It's been one of those days,' Tomkin said, as Paddy Joe sighed. 'Never mind. Better luck tomorrow. Start Storm's lessons again, in the morning before we go off to Scotland, and we'll get him straight during the holiday, Paddy Joe. He must learn not to be disobedient. Especially as he's an Alsatian. They're big headstrong dogs and like their own way and they must learn they can't have it. A lot of people are afraid of them, like that bus conductor. Some of them come from bad breeding and they earn the others a bad name. But it's not only Alsatians that have bad blood. The worst dog I ever knew was a Jack Russell. Kill a fox as soon as look at it, would Rip, but he tried his teeth on people too, and that was that. Dogs are only allowed one bite, Paddy Joe. And if your dog's a bad dog it's not his fault. It's yours.'

Paddy Joe knew that. He knew that he should have

given Storm his lessons, but somehow, now that he was back in his old home, with the Colonel and Tomkin instead of Grandee and Martha, he felt adrift. And he had run wild for two whole weeks, without any adults to tell him what to do. Lessons, both for himself and for Storm, were irksome. It was much more fun to play, and Storm had been rebellious and difficult to handle. Paddy Joe did not realise that the dog was bewildered too, and missed his grandmother, who had looked after him and fed him when Paddy Joe was at school. Now Storm only had one firmly rationed meal a day, instead of two, and he had to wait for Paddy Joe to give it to him, and worst of all, Grandee had vanished. She had always come back before, and the dog often ran to the gate and watched the road outside, waiting for her. No one could tell him that she would never come again and his memory of people he loved was vivid. He only forgot the things he was made to do against his own will.

It was the Colonel who realised that Paddy Joe and the dog were fretting, and suggested that they all went away for a short spell, back to Scotland, to resume the fishing holiday which he had interrupted when he saw the notice of Grandee's death in the newspaper. It would help both the boy and the dog and perhaps when they came home again the memories would be less painful. Term had begun, but the headmaster was understanding, and Paddy Joe had promised to make up the lessons that he would miss.

Paddy Joe had never been to Scotland. Tomkin told him about the island on which they were to stay, about the mountains and the sea lochs where the herons fished and the weed was orange-red and seals basked on the rocks. It was a wonderful place, the island, Tomkin said, and had everything. Roe deer and red deer. Pine marten and kestrel. Badger and fox. Paddy Joe felt he couldn't wait.

He hated towns. Towns bored him. He liked being out of doors, walking with his dog. When Grandee was alive he often visited the Colonel, who was always talking about fishing, and Tomkin took Paddy Joe into the woods and taught him how to stalk, and how to move silently in the trees, and how not to cast a shadow. Tomkin also taught him how to shoot, and once took him to a clay pigeon shoot, and Paddy Joe vowed that one day he too would be a champion, like Tomkin, who won every event that night.

But Tomkin was a hard taskmaster. When Paddy Joe had finished his homework and fed his dog, he had to make ready his own equipment; had to check his fishing line and oil the gears on the reel; had to inspect his rod and sort out hooks and weights and traces; had to mend the tent he was to sleep in, in the cottage garden, when the nights were fine. Tomkin made him undo the first patch and do it again.

'That'll leak. You do it proper, Paddy Joe, and never give up.'

Tomkin was a lean brown little man with a lophlipped grin and fierce blue eyes and eyebrows that bristled above them. He had the tireless walk of the shepherd, and he knew more about the country than anyone Paddy Joe had ever met. He knew the ways of foxes and where the badger dug in the wood, he had heard yound kestrels crying for food, and climbed the rock to the eagle's eyrie and looked down on its ugly fledgling. He had a fund of stories, and he helped Paddy Joe teach Storm his manners.

'I've no use for an ill-mannered pup, and it makes a useless dog, Paddy Joe,' Tomkin said, when Grandee bought the dog. Each day they trained Storm, teaching him to sit and stay until he was released, to come when he was called, to go down, and to walk to heel. Storm remembered his lessons so long as he was reminded

14

daily, but once forget and Storm forgot too. He only remembered the things he wanted to remember.

'Never give up, Paddy Joe.'

Sometimes Paddy Joe thought the phrase would be written on his brain. But it was useful to remember and often when he was tired or things seemed too difficult Tomkin's soft voice sounded in his ears again. 'Never give up.'

It was much easier to give up. Much easier to say 'I can't,' than 'I can.' Much easier to leave jobs undone and go away and find something more interesting to do, but it was never allowed. Paddy Joe had to learn and Tomkin saw that he did learn.

Tomkin put aside the paper and started making lists. He was always well organised. Even the Colonel was excited. He was whistling to himself as he worked. The big dining table was covered with rods and artificial flies and fishing line and fishing reels and a small bottle of oil stood neatly on a folded newspaper. The Colonel was inspecting hooks. A copy of the *Lord of the Rings* lay on the little table. It had been Grandee's favourite book. Paddy Joe suddenly missed her intensely; he missed her soft voice, and her teasing fun, and her gentleness. Both Tomkin and the Colonel were kind, but now there was no gentleness. Nothing was the same, and the Colonel was too busy to notice Paddy Joe, who picked up the book and slipped out of the room again, careful to make no sound. There was a lump in his throat that refused to be swallowed. He was lonely for Grandee and the life that he used to lead and he felt that he did not belong, anywhere.

Storm came padding out of the kitchen, looking for Paddy Joe. He too was uneasy and could not understand why Grandee had vanished. He had gone off that morning, looking for her, trying to see if he could find her in her former haunts.

15

It was not until after their holiday that Tomkin discovered that the dog had wandered forlornly from shop to shop, hunting for his dead mistress; had waited outside the doctor's house, looking at the people leaving the surgery, and then, tail drooping, had taken the road to school, wanting Paddy Joe, finding the house too strange, with men there who did not belong. Tomkin regretted his anger with boy and dog, and realised suddenly how they must have felt, but by then it was too late to do more than try to make amends. The harsh words had already been said.

Paddy Joe called to Storm, who followed the boy upstairs. It was the one concession that the Colonel made, and the dog slept on the floor beside the boy's bed. No one slept in Grandee's room. The Colonel and Tomkin both had rooms at the back of the house. The dog stopped at the door, as he stopped every night, and looked at Paddy Joe, and Paddy Joe looked back. He could never tell the Alsatian that Grandee had gone and he knew that her room still smelled of her, and that the dog remembered her as vividly as if she were there.

Storm whined and scratched at the door with his paw and Paddy Joe opened it. Tomkin, coming up the stairs to fetch a pen from his room, saw them, and stopped. He had not seen this night-time routine before. Paddy Joe stood in the doorway, his face shadowed. The dog went inside and sniffed all round the empty room. He sniffed at the wardrobe and the bed, and came out again, his tail drooping. Paddy Joe was blinded by tears and even Tomkin was forced to blink and swallow. He waited until Paddy Joe was in bed and went into the boy's room, pretending he had seen nothing. He was annoyed with himself for not thinking more about the boy.

He sat beside Paddy Joe for a short time and talked of Scotland; of the long journey ahead, of the hills and the

16

creatures that lived in them. Paddy Joe went to sleep with his head full of dreams and woke to find day shining behind the apple tree, and dressed and ran into the garden, unable to stay in bed.

He romped with Storm and remembered to give the dog a brief lesson, but it had little value as neither could concentrate. He rolled with the Alsatian in the grass and threw a ball and they stopped playing at last, breathless. Storm rescued an ancient bone, that he had buried beneath the tree, and gnawed it while Paddy Joe climbed into the fork between the lower branches and bit on a ripe red apple and felt excitement build to a pitch that was almost unendurable. He longed to run and shout, but he stayed quiet, holding down impatience, and wondered how everyone else could sleep when they were to start their journey so soon. He thought that they would never wake.

2

Scotland was pure delight. They travelled in brilliant sunshine that heightened colour; the heather was in flower, and purple contrasted with the dull green. They arrived to find the sea quiet under an opalescent sky darkened by low cloud on the horizon. Paddy Joe wanted to explore, but he had to help unload the car and unpack the cases, and prepare a meal, and feed Storm.

Paddy Joe ate his supper and then wandered round the rooms. The cottage fascinated him. It was built of stone, and very old. Black rafters crossed the ceilings. There was a vast ghostly cupboard under the creaking stairs and each bedroom was furnished with old-fashioned wardrobes and chests. Tomkin had a brass bedstead so busy with ornament that the metal spheres touched one another all along five rails. The ends were furbished with enormous domed knobs that unscrewed. Paddy Joe took one off, hoping to find a secret message inside, but there was only dust. Tomkin, coming into the room and seeing it, made Paddy Joe take a damp cloth and clean the hollows so that he wished he had not bothered to investigate.

Two hours later rain was drenching from sullen clouds that seemed to hang above the chimneys. The Colonel had gone out after supper to try to catch fish on the evening rise, in a little stream on the mainland. He came home soaked and ill-tempered, because there were no fish in the river, he said crossly. He bathed in a vast tin bath in front of the kitchen fire, while Tomkin boiled water in enormous pans and Paddy Joe cooled it with kettles full of cold water, and the Colonel soaked the aches from his bones.

He recovered his temper when Tomkin cooked hot soup, instead of the usual bedtime drink, and, because it was the first night of the holiday and everyone was excited, they sat on while the wood fire burned in the big old hearth and Storm listened to the noises outside in the night, his head cocked, his ears pricked, his eyes alive with interest.

There was a pile of cut wood in the outhouse, and Paddy Joe lay on the hearthrug, watching the blaze. Sparks flew up the chimney and he saw pictures in the flames. A real fire was luxury. There were exciting caves among the ashes, and dancing flickers that flared and died, and different colours; blue, yellow, violet and red, a perpetual firework display, especially vivid when a log slipped, and glared again in a sudden flurry.

Tomkin was sitting at a rickety wooden table, tying flies, his face intent as he concentrated. The piles of feathers and fine wires were close to his hand and Paddy Joe grinned to himself when Tomkin breathed deeply, because the feathers blew across the table and Tomkin exclaimed irritably. The flies came alive under his deft fingers; blue and brown and gold, incredible imitations that looked more real than the flies that danced on the water.

'Weather changes fast here,' Tomkin commented, as wind shook the chimney and roared in the trees. 'You can see the storms building on the horizon and racing across the water. They come so sudden in the mountains you have to watch. It doesn't do to take a boat out on the loch unless you've looked at the weather. Have to learn to read the sky. Weather forecasts are no good here. It only tells you there's a gale when the gale's on you. Hark at that. You'd never believe it was so quiet when we arrived, only three hours ago.'

The clock struck eleven. Paddy Joe had no desire to go to bed. He could sleep late in the morning, and he would never sleep now, he knew. He hoped that the Colonel and Tomkin would fail to notice the time. They were not as anxious as Grandee had been to see he went to bed early. It was a long time since either had lived with a boy.

Outside the window the wind screamed, and waves roared on the beach, which was only a few hundred yards away, across a field and over a little stone-built wall. Paddy Joe rolled over on his back and looked up at the black beams. He wondered who had lived in the cottage and how old it was. He knew it had belonged to the steward who had managed the estate, but the man at the garage had told Tomkin on a former visit that the cottage was far older than the other houses on the island and had been there long before the Great House had been built.

Perhaps there were ghosts, thought Paddy Joe. Or hidden treasure. The door creaked and opened in a draught from the window and Paddy Joe jumped and Storm leaped to his feet and barked and everyone laughed as Tomkin soothed the dog. The Alsatian sat down again sheepishly, but cocked his head, as if he were listening to footsteps in the shadows. Paddy Joe looked out into the dark hall, and hoped that he would not have to cross it alone on his way to bed. There was no electric light. A hurricane lamp lit the room.

'Bed soon, Paddy Joe,' the Colonel said, tamping tobacco firmly into the curved pipe that he always smoked. His white hair was short and neatly cut; his white moustache was silky and trim and brushed, a sharp contrast to a skin tanned by his outdoor life. He walked and fished and rode, and spent little time indoors. Now his riding days were over, as he had sold his two hunters. He could not afford to keep them, with a boy to bring up. Paddy Joe was sorry that they had gone, but he did not guess the reason, and the Colonel and Tomkin took care that he never knew that his coming had made a difference to their way of life. Grandee had not been rich and the Colonel lived on an army pension.

'One story first,' the Colonel said, and Paddy Joe settled himself with his back against Storm, who was stretched out sleepily on the hearthrug, eyes half open, as he tried to identify the odd noises outside. The crash of waves mystified him, but he was used to wind in the trees.

'Stories,' the Colonel repeated. 'I used to love story hour at home. I had four brothers and a sister, and we went to my mother's sitting-room every evening, and she either read to us or told us about her mother, and the things she'd done when she was a girl. My grandfather lived in a house near the river, and when the river flooded they had to carry everything out of harm's way and live upstairs until the water went down again. Once it came so high they all had to be taken out of the house through one of the bedroom windows into a boat. They had horses and cattle and pigs, so that the very first sign of flood water meant driving all the stock to high ground. It must have been very exciting, but my mother said it always happened in winter and all she remembered was being cold!'

'Was her house as old as this one?' Paddy Joe asked.

The Colonel shook his head.

'Old Mac says this one was built when Charles the First was on the English throne. It's seen all kinds of exciting events. They say that Prince Charlie hid here once, but I don't think that's true. I don't believe he was ever in these parts, but he's supposed to have slept in Tomkin's bed.'

'It's old enough, and uncomfortable enough,' Tomkin said. 'I reckon they stuffed it with nuts and bolts. Oh, drat the feathers!' he added crossly as his breath blew them across the table again.

'I'll tell you who did live here,' the Colonel said. 'A man called the Black Hermit, because of his black beard and his black temper.'

'A hermit?' asked Paddy Joe.

'A bit of everything,' said the Colonel. 'He was an unlucky man. He lived here just before the French Revolution, and at that time he had a new pretty wife and a baby girl. Then, one night, there was a great storm, and his wife, coming through the woods with her arms full of firewood, was killed by a falling tree. He wanted nothing more to do with people after that. He and his little daughter lived here, and saw no one. There was no one to compel a child to go to school, and in any case I doubt if there would have been a school here, so the Black Hermit and little Morag lived entirely alone.'

'Not seeing anyone?' asked Paddy Joe. It sounded a very dull way to live.

'Morag had a dog. A dog like Storm. She loved him more than any other creature and she grew up with him. When he died she became a little strange and spent much of her time singing to the seals on the beaches.'

Paddy Joe thought of Morag, growing up on the island, walking in the woods with her dog, as he walked in the woods. He wondered if she trained her dog, or let him run free. He looked into the flames, and tried to picture her, slender, with long fair hair, running along the beach, an Alsatian like Storm beside her; or lying in the sunshine, singing to the seals.

'One day a young fisherman, fishing off the shore, heard her singing and came to talk to her,' the Colonel said. 'He came again, and again. Until her father saw him, and shot at him. He escaped, but the Hermit warned his daughter that if she saw him again, he would kill the fisherman. The fisherman came back one night, and Morag, who by now was grown up, agreed to run away with him. Five nights later he came for her. The sea was smooth when he came but by dark a storm had come up from the hills, just as it has tonight, and the wild wind shrieked through the trees, and the young fisherman lay in the wet woods waiting. Morag joined him. Her father saw her go, and followed her. They pushed the heavy boat off from the shore. The Hermit shouted to them to stop, but his voice was lost in the howl of the wind, and the crash of the breakers on the shore. No one ever saw either of them again.'

'What happened?' Paddy Joe asked. He felt sorry for the lovers, rowing off into the storm rather than face the Hermit's rage. He knew how they felt. He hated facing Tomkin when he was angry.

'No one knows,' the Colonel said. 'Some said they escaped the storm, and rowed ashore, far away, and went to live in England. Whatever happened the Hermit lived alone here until his death, feeding on the wild creatures that he trapped, seeing no one and speaking to no one. They say he was a huge old man, and by then, though he was still known as the Black Hermit, he had a long grey beard and long grey hair and fierce eyes. He shot at everyone who came to the island, so people left him alone. Children ran from him when he went to town.'

Paddy Joe, looking into the flames, thought that if ever a place was haunted, this deserved to be; by Morag, singing softly to the seals, and by her dog, and by the fierce old man, living his lonely desolate life, hating the world and everyone in it. The screaming wind was the Black Hermit shouting his rage.

23

The wind, blustering ferociously through the trees, shook the cottage. Somewhere in the wood a branch broke, the sound echoing like a cannon shot. Storm ran to the window and put his paws on the sill and looked out and barked. Everything was strange here. He came back to Paddy Joe, needing familiarity. Paddy Joe looked out too, but all he could see was the reflection of the room, bright against the night. It was too windy to sleep in his tent in the garden. Tomkin had promised he could use the tent when the weather was fine—perhaps tomorrow.

'Bed,' Tomkin said. 'And tomorrow, immediately after breakfast, we must give Storm a lesson. He must learn to come when he's called. It wouldn't do to lose him here. There are far too many dangers and he's not used to the sea.'

The passage outside the room was as dark as Paddy Joe had feared and the wooden stairs creaked. Paddy Joe was sure that footsteps followed him. He stopped twice to listen, aware that Storm's fur was bristling, and that the dog was growling deep in his throat. It was frightening to know that you could not banish darkness with the click of a switch and that the shadows would only disappear when morning brought daylight. The rooms were unfamiliar, and Paddy Joe hit his shin painfully on his bed. He was thankful that Storm was beside him. He reached his hand to fondle the dog's ears and Storm licked the boy's wrist and curled up with a deep sigh and went to sleep, and his breathing was a comfort in the room, and audible above the noises of the wind.

Paddy Joe slept and dreamed of a girl who ran along the beach, an Alsatian dog jumping up at her side. Storm lay with his nose on his paws, listening, his ears alert. Every smell was new to him, and outside were scents that roused age-old instincts. He could not rest.

3

It was three in the morning when Storm loped to the window. There was scent on the night-time air; scent of a bird roosting peacefully in the eaves; scent of the house martin's nest beside the window, a neat bowl of mud, plastered into shape, and lined with moss. That scent was only a memory, for the birds had flown and the autumn rain was washing away the fabric of the nest that now clung forlornly to the window embrasure.

There were other scents and he sniffed, and pricked his ears, listening; sea wrack and sea spume, salty and tangy; a tree smelling of resin, close to the window, and over it, sharp, rank, unbearably exciting, came the musky odour of a fox.

Fox! Storm growled deep in his throat. Running fox, hunting fox, night-time prowling fox, hungry fox, wolf-like fox, red brush waving, red mouth gaping, red body hungering for food.

Paddy Joe woke, and called the dog, who came reluctantly, and nosed his master, telling him that there were travellers abroad in the night. There was no response, as Paddy Joe was already asleep again, dreaming of a dark cave in which he could see nothing and was trapped, and through his dream a giant beast came running, hot breath slavering, huge paws tearing, so that Paddy Joe shouted aloud, and Tomkin put his head round the door.

'Nightmare trotting?' he asked, sympathetic, and Paddy Joe sat up, and shook his head to reassure himself. This had only been a dream and he was awake.

'Then let's have a midnight prowl and a bit of a bite,' Tomkin said.

It was adventure to walk through the dark cottage, to pass the door of the room where the Colonel slept, creeping barefoot on the shiny boards, Storm walking behind, aware that he must not make a noise either. Soft-footed down the creaking stairs, soft-footed through the dining-room where the moonlit chairs were alien and unfriendly.

The kitchen fire still glowed faintly, and Tomkin flung wood on to it so that it blazed and crackled and drove away the dark. Soon he was making hot chocolate, and Paddy Joe was tucking into biscuits, and Storm had found his old bone and was chewing away at it, enjoying wide-awake human company at such an unearthly hour. The night beckoned at the uncurtained windows, and the shifting branches of trees, lit by a far away faint moon, shivered in the wind.

It was easy to dream of magic; of witches abroad on their broomsticks, of black cats yowling over the walls, of hidden and secret and unguessable deeds done under cover of night. Paddy Joe shivered, but not with cold. He watched the flames, and thought of an armour-clad knight galloping to fight a dragon that devoured everything that lay before it. Perhaps in olden times it had been easier and safer to think of dragons and demons and hob-goblins, rather than plague and pestilence, and the scaring things that men could do when they've a mind.

'No use sitting there getting the willy wambles,' Tomkin said. 'You and me'll be seeing things next. I could'a sworn there was someone in the garden and Storm's been seeing ghosties all evening. Just look at him now.'

26

Storm had heard a noise in the distance, a far away panic noise. His brown eyes turned first towards Tomkin and then to Paddy Joe, as if he could not believe that they were so insensitive that they could not hear the screams that filled the air, or sense the terror that was beating against the darkness, as close as if it were in the garden outside.

It was useless. They heard nothing and never understood. Storm followed Paddy Joe upstairs again and curled nose to tail on the rug by the bed, but his ears listened, and the fur of his ruff was a-bristle till dawn, when the fear soothed out in the newborn light, and the air was still again.

Had Tomkin and Paddy Joe looked, they would have seen the fox circle the garden, and then go on to the farm. None of the farm dogs scented him. The wind blew from him to the hills behind, and blew from the farm to the fox and told him of chicken. The smell of chicken wet his mouth and saliva ran down his beard and he quickened his pace.

There had not been foxes on the farm for many years. The wire was neglected and in one place the pegs had eased, and the old red rebel was through, his lips opened in anticipation.

The hens were quiet. The inner hut was not so easy, but Reynard was hungry and hunger knew no caution. He worried the wire that held the latch with teeth and nose, until it worked loose, and the latch slipped, and he was inside, and so was pandemonium.

The chickens were isolated in small cages, and guarding them was Larrie, the sheepdog, trusted and trustworthy, and his boon companion, Tay, an evil-tempered and extremely large gander.

The great bird ran at the fox, hissing furiously, his anger boundless, his courage far bigger than his brain.

Reynard had never seen a goose before, let alone a

gander, racing towards him, neck outstretched and beak snapping. This creature smelled of bird, but was no meek chicken, and the fox fell back into the doorway. The wind blew the door shut behind him. He was trapped, and at the mercy of both dog and gander. The chickens squawked, clucking shrilly in terror the great white bird ran round the fox's legs, little black eyes sparkling with hate, and Larrie, with a low deep-throated growl, sprang.

The fox tried to get out of the door. The noise in the small space terrified him. He was caged with panic, and the snarling mouth pierced him in a dozen places, inflicting bite after bite on his unprotected body. The gander raced round both of the animals, darting in his beak whenever he had a chance.

The fox dared not turn his attention from the dog to snap at the gander. Larrie was enormous, a rough-bred collie built for ferocity, able to battle with fox and eagle, and more of a protector than a herd-dog for the sheep. His little quiet mate, Mara, was the herd-dog. Larrie was kept in the field all night when lambs were on the hills, and he was used to fighting. Now he had the advantage of familiar territory. He fought quietly, using his powerful teeth to grab and hold, but was forced again and again to let go and dodge the snapping jaws. Reynard was no flee-fighter, and, were he ever trapped by a hound pack, would battle dearly for his life. No one near could have slept through the din. The farmer grabbed his coat and snatched his gun, and raced to the hencoop, where he loaded fast, with an expertise born of long practice. He was too wise a gunman ever to carry a loaded weapon. He'd known one man shoot himself in the foot, and another trip and near blind a friend, and it wasn't worth it, not for the extra seconds. Better to let the quarry escape than to end a human life.

He opened the door of the hencoop and the fox made

a dash for freedom, bolting between the man's legs, so that in spite of all his foresight he went sprawling and the gun went off, killing the gander which was running to chase off the intruder.

The farmwife ran into the yard and helped her husband to his feet, upbraiding him, while he swore furiously. He sent Larrie after the fox, and looked down bitterly at the corpse of old Tay. They'd have to eat him for dinner, and that was an ill reward for the poor creature, that had only been doing his duty, and paid the wrong price. There was no justice in the world at all.

There was no time either, for Larrie had turned the fox, which came like a red streak through the farmyard. The farmer lifted his gun, vengeance in his mind, but dog and fox were now fighting by the farmyard wall, the moon showing every detail clear, as they tumbled and bit, past the dark shapes of plough and harrow, and thumped against the barn, snarling and snapping.

Suddenly the fox was uppermost and the dog was rolling on his back in the midden, trying to free himself from the cloying stinking heap. He was thigh deep and floundering, and the fox leapt the wall, and was away, running like a shadow up the hill. The farmer whistled the dog as it extricated itself, and Larrie came slowly, his legs stiff, his tail wagging.

'Never mind, lad. You did your best,' the man said, knowing praise was due and the dog would feel he had failed, as the fox had got away.

'He'll need a bath in the morning,' the farmwife said. It meant another chore, as the sheepdogs were rarely bathed, but Larrie was not fit to be smelled. The dog went back to the henhouse and lay across the door. He had seen the gander's body, and his tail went down. They'd had good times together, he and Tay, playing absurd games of tag round the haystacks, ever since Tay was a small and bedraggled gosling, rescued in his turn from one of the farm cats who had disgraced himself by hunting the farm birds, and been given away to a family without such temptations.

Next day, when Paddy Joe went for the milk, he saw Larrie being bathed in the sheepdip trough, his tail down, his face hangdog, and heard the story of the thief in the night. Tomkin, who had come with him, looked at Storm.

'It's a pity you can't talk,' he told the dog. 'You knew there was trouble afoot last night, didn't you, feller?'

Storm wagged his tail. He had no idea what Tomkin was talking about, but he was delighted to have any attention from the humans who lived with him. His big mouth opened and his lips went back, and Paddy Joe laughed, sure his dog was grinning.

4

The Colonel drove off as soon as breakfast was finished, and Tomkin mapped out the day for himself and Paddy Joe. Vegetables to dig up from the little kitchen garden that the landlord kept stocked for the benefit of his summer visitors. There were potatoes and carrots and turnips and a few late runner beans, all ready for use when they were needed. There were blackberries on the island and Paddy Joe was sent to pick them for supper. Then it was time for Storm's training session. He was becoming very disobedient, with a will of his own.

Storm did not want his lesson. The island was too exciting. There were all kinds of smells and he wanted to hunt, and Paddy Joe had skimped his training for nearly five weeks. Storm walked to heel when Tomkin made him obey, but he kept turning his head, and he pulled away from Paddy Joe, resenting the leash. He would not walk at heel without the leash either, but dashed off to sniff down a rabbit hole, and to bark at a squirrel, and Tomkin took over the training completely, as he was afraid that the dog might endanger himself by disobedience.

Storm sat, but sat askew, his tongue lolling. He was not working. He was playing the fool and when told to go down he rolled on his back and waved his paws in the air and Paddy Joe laughed and Tomkin was angry. Laughter made the dog worse. He would play to the gallery, clowning. But it was difficult to keep a straight face.

The session was not a success, and Tomkin decreed that as Storm kept running off, he should be put on the leash again, and perhaps that would make him remember his manners. Paddy Joe knew how the dog felt. He was impatient too. Tomkin had promised they should go fishing, but it seemed that the time would never come.

At last they were out in the fibre-glass dinghy that the Colonel had hired. The waves were flecked with white foam. Storm, sitting in the bows, watched the fishing line intently as it streamed from the reel, the spinner twisting behind it, glinting in the sun.

The line twitched, and Storm barked.

Tomkin, holding the tiller of the little outboard motor, laughed. His brown face creased in a lophlipped grin, and his greying hair, ruffled in the breeze, stood up spikily.

'Who's fishing? You, or the dog?' he asked, and Paddy Joe grinned. Storm barked every time they hooked a mackerel. Paddy Joe tested the line. It was dancing vigorously. He began to pull it in, not sure at first whether he had a catch, or was merely entangled with seaweed. The line jerked. A mackerel leaped high, attempted to break free, landed heavily in the water, and dashed away from the boat.

The line was alive, tugging, twisting, spinning off the reel. Paddy Joe braked. The fish fought against the pull that brought it closer to the dinghy. It began to tire. The struggles were less, and Paddy Joe reeled in. Storm, tail waving, watched expectantly, and sniffed the fish as it lay on the floor, twitching even after Tomkin had killed it with a sharp blow on the head. It was the third fish that they had caught that afternoon. The mackerel were shoaling, and the edge of the loch was alive with tiny fry that had fled into shallow water to avoid the barred predators that fed on them.

'Time to go,' Tomkin said. Paddy Joe stretched

cramped arms and legs, and pushed dark strands of straight hair from nutmeg-brown eyes, and eased clenched sun tanned fingers. He put away his rod. He looked about him; at the loch, surrounded by mountains down which pine trees marched in endless procession; at the rocky beach where a hoodie crow turned over the brown-gold sea-wrack, searching for food; at the sky, where black clouds, streaked with scarlet, laced the green and golden streamers that pointed to the setting sun.

'Wind again tonight,' Tomkin said, 'It's often windy here. Last night was nothing compared to some gales I've known. The Colonel and I once chartered a small yacht and fished from that, on this loch, and we were marooned aboard for three days. It was far too rough to risk coming ashore.'

Paddy Joe was not sure that he would enjoy being marooned on a small boat in rough weather. The waves were choppy now and he felt very slightly sick and would be glad to reach land again.

'See those streamers?' Tomkin said, pointing to the sky. 'Wind'll come in the early dawn and tomorrow it will blow much too hard for fishing. You'll see.'

Paddy Joe was sure he would see. Tomkin knew all about weather. He had a countryman's sense for it, as well aware as any shepherd of impending change. Storm was aware of weather change too, and would lift his head and sniff before rain as if he could smell a difference in the air. Perhaps he could at that, Paddy Joe thought.

'The marsh over there is a Nature Reserve.' Tomkin pointed to the spit of land that lay on their beam. 'There are all kinds of rare butterflies; and a kestrel's nest in the big tree. I heard the little ones squeaking when we were here in the spring.'

'There's a rocky outcrop beyond the point, where the water's white,' he went on. 'Watch for changes in the look of the surface. Out at sea, breaking waves are a sign of

33

rocks or sandbanks, or some hidden obstruction. You can see a tide race too. You can't ever relax, when you're boating. It's not like being on land.'

Paddy Joe looked towards the shore as they motored towards a deserted jetty that lifted gaunt iron beams from the surging water.

'I think we'll be safer landing on the beach,' Tomkin said.

Paddy Joe noticed broken ends and protruding iron bars. He pointed to a sandy spit that shelved gently. They dragged the boat above high water mark, removed the outboard motor and the oars and carried her to lie snug against an old stone wall, upside down to keep her dry from rain.

The fields beyond the grassy edge of the beach were thistle sown and sorrel seeded. Years before, they had been farmed, had grown crops and grazed cattle, and chickens had scurried and scraped in the yards.

Paddy Joe stumbled and tripped over a rock. He was carrying his life jacket and the oars. Tomkin had not removed his life jacket, as the outboard motor was heavy and needed both hands. Paddy Joe also had his rod, tucked awkwardly under his arm, and Storm walked proudly, the baler held in his jaws. He enjoyed helping carry their possessions, and often at home, if he had nothing else to bring, would carry Paddy Joe's old school cap, sure he was contributing to everyone's pleasure.

Paddy Joe looked at the stone pillars that framed the empty gateway. They leaned towards each other confidentially. Beyond was the bridge causeway, spanning the roaring tide. At low water they could cross to the mainland, over the rocks and patches of sand.

'It's hard to believe people once lived here and it was all cared for, isn't it?' Paddy Joe looked at the rocky beach, showing through the trees. Beyond it, covered in coarse grass, was the outline of the road that must once have led to the jetty. There was no trace of gravel on the drive. Brambles stretched thorny tentacles, blurring the verges, and many of the paths were hidden in a tangle of undergrowth.

'You have to watch the boggy places,' Tomkin said, 'It's treacherous going.'

He pointed out the signs of bog; grasses tipped with cottontails; soft soggy cushions of yellow green bogmoss that squelched water when they were pressed. Underneath the earth was black and sour and peaty.

A bird croaked suddenly in the long grass.

'Corncrake,' Tomkin said. 'That's one you can't mistake.'

They had reached the cottage. The Colonel waited in the doorway, a broad grin on his face and two large salmon in his hand.

'Never rains but it pours,' Tomkin said, flinging down the mackerel which he had strung together and tied to his belt to make them easy to carry.

'We'll smoke those,' the Colonel said. 'I bet you've never smoked fish, eh, Paddy Joe?'

Tomkin took the salmon and went to the kitchen to clean it, while Paddy Joe began to collect wood. There was dead wood everywhere; dry thin sticks and large lichened chunks that were rotten and fell apart in a mist of brown wood; thick twigs and broken branches, and chips left by someone who had felled a tree. Soon they had a large pile ready to burn and the Colonel made a tripod and spitted the split mackerel so that they hung above the smoke. Paddy Joe watched, fascinated.

Tomkin prepared a feast for supper. He brought it outside, and they ate by the woodfire. They ate salmon dressed with parsley, and late runner beans, and potatoes, mashed with the milk which Paddy Joe fetched from the farm in the morning. They ate blackberries, and cream from the top of the milk, and the sun slid behind the mountains and the moon hung over them. Tomkin stretched out on the ground.

'Like old times eh, Colonel?' he said, and the Colonel nodded, remembering the many camps during the war when they had fared much worse than this and fed on scraps saved from other meals, and tinned corned beef and stale dry biscuits.

Far away, beyond the steward's house, a bird called in sudden alarm. Storm sat up, his ears listening, his nose asking the wind for news. He pawed Paddy Joe's leg eagerly, but Paddy Joe did not understand, and only the dog knew that a vixen had passed on the hill, her scent blown towards them.

'I wonder what's bothering the birds,' the Colonel said lazily. Storm was telling him, but none of them understood. The Alsatian settled himself in the dusk, nose on paws, aware of many things hidden from human noses. The wind that Tomkin had promised strengthened slightly, and whined in the trees above them, but it was quiet enough to sleep outside. Tomkin helped Paddy Joe put up the little tent in the cottage garden.

The Colonel and Tomkin removed the mackerel and doused the fire, while Paddy Joe crawled wearily into his sleeping bag. Storm stretched out on the groundsheet beside him. Paddy Joe left the tentflap open so that he could watch the brilliant stars. The owl hooted again, the vixen barked, Storm pricked his ears, and a car on the mainland changed gear and was gone. Paddy Joe slept. Storm left his side and prowled the garden, distracted by the night-time scents and sounds, and hunting instincts that had long lain dormant roused inside him, so that he found it hard to obey when Paddy Joe woke and called him. He sighed deeply and settled, nose on paws, and quivered with repressed excitement.

5

Day was only a rumour when Storm woke, barking.
Paddy Joe roused himself sleepily. There were footsteps
on the drive. A soft Scots voice spoke to the dog, and
Storm hesitated, uncertain.

Paddy Joe crawled out of the tent, and looked in
astonishment at the two men who stood there, smiling at
him placatingly.

'We will not do you any harm, young master,' one of
them said.

Paddy Joe suddenly realised that he knew who they
were. He had heard about them from the farmer. Mac
and Andy loved pheasant and grouse, rabbit and
salmon. They loved the rivers and the woods, but they
had never loved work.

When magistrates sat, there, only too often, were the
pair of reprobates, waiting, smiles of hopeful recogni-
tion on their bearded faces. Mac was tall, black haired,
black bearded and invariably dressed in a long black
overcoat that fitted too tightly across his brawny chest.
His eyes looked merrily out of a thatch of hair that hid
the rest of his face. He loved singing and he always sang
hymns. Andy was smaller, spare figured, his hair and
beard less luxuriant, a bright gleaming red that out-
shone the sun.

He rarely laughed, but he possessed a dry sardonic
humour that caused several magistrates to hide smiles

with their hands, and give a lesser penance than they at first intended. Mac and Andy took their punishment like men, admitting they deserved it, but the call of wood and river was too strong, and all too often they came back. Mac was bold. But Andy was fearful—a superstitious man who never walked under a ladder, and took care not to look over his left shoulder at the new moon through glass.

For once they had no misdeed in mind. They had met the Colonel on his previous visits to the island, and had come in their rickety old car to see how he fared and to see the lad and the dog as well. They liked lads, and they liked dogs, and the village policeman had said that the Alsatian was exceptionally well trained and intelligent.

Their car stood on the overgrown drive, and Paddy Joe looked at it in disbelief. Andy had bought it from a travelling tinker for ten pounds. The mudguards and number plates were held on with odd bits of wire and frayed string, the doors were loose, and when Andy wished to stop he took his feet off the accelerator, allowing the car to slow under its own momentum until it reached walking pace. Then Mac jumped out and pushed two baulks of wood under the wheels.

'We do not take it on the roads, ye ken,' Mac said apologetically, following Paddy Joe's glance.

'Only where the roads cross the lanes,' explained Andy, who, though not exactly honest, was always truthful.

'We came to look for Mr Tomkin, and we brought some food to make a change for ye,' Andy said. 'Maybe the Colonel will remember us when he catches him a fine fat salmon,' he added.

Tomkin came out of the cottage, having heard their voices. He grinned when he saw them.

'I see you've introduced yourselves,' he said. 'You'd better get dressed, Paddy Joe.'

Mac and Andy followed Tomkin into the kitchen. Dressing was only the work of a moment. Paddy Joe rinsed his face and hands hurriedly in the water butt which collected rain water from the roof gutters, and pulled on jeans and shirt, and combed his hair. He walked inside to find Tomkin admiring a fat duck, while the Colonel looked at it with a quizzical expression, wondering how the pair of poachers had come by it.

'It would be a wild duck, wandering, and belonging to no one, Colonel,' Andy explained. 'It has a fish hook in it, and it was cruel to let it live. Some careless fisherman must have left his trace and bait and the puir duck ate it, and was in considerable pain.'

'We have asked everywhere who has lost a fine duck with a fish hook in its mouth, but nobody owns it,' Mac said virtuously. The Colonel laughed.

'You'd better share our breakfast in return,' he said.

'We hoped for that,' said Mac. 'We have brought some bacon with us to contribute our share, and guinea fowl eggs from Mistress Cameron at the farm, with her compliments, and thanks for the fish you brought her yesterday. And there's a pair of nice rabbits will make a Huntsman's stew for you.'

'The rabbits just fell into your pockets,' Tomkin said.

'Indeed they did not,' said Andy. 'We shot them on the island. We said we would bring them to the Colonel, as he has shooting rights on the island. It is not poaching as we have brought him his own property and saved him the trouble of hunting it for himself.'

The Colonel looked at the two men and shook his head at them.

'One rabbit for you and one for me,' he said. 'We can't eat all that and there's no refrigerator here.'

'That was what we thought,' Andy said. 'We hoped that you might let us keep one rabbit. It was a pity to let it run, as it was such an easy shot, and asking to be taken, and there are still too many rabbits on the island. Myxamatosis has never reached here, the Lord be praised.'

Breakfast was eaten with more laughter than Paddy Joe remembered in his life. Mac and Andy were full of amusing tales, many of them of animals that lived on or near the island. Their world was a simple one, and the affairs of the birds and beasts were as enthralling to them as the backstreet gossip of a busy city to the city dwellers.

'If you want to know about beasts, you want to come with us at night,' Andy said. Paddy Joe turned to look at the Colonel, who nodded.

'You won't come to any harm,' he said. 'Only one thing. Don't you dare take the boy poaching. I won't stand for that'

'We would not dream of such a thing,' Andy said virtuously. 'We may not always obey the law ourselves, but it would be a wicked thing indeed to teach a young gentleman to break it. You must learn to be much better than we are, young sir. We had not the benefit of your excellent schooling.'

The day seemed suddenly endless when Andy and Mac had gone. Paddy Joe watched the clouds shut off the sun, and walked on the beach, where it was grey and bleak and lonely. Tomkin had taken the boat out to fish in deep waters, and wanted to be alone. Five seals lay on Seal Rock, sleeping, but there was no other sign of life except for wheeling, quarrelling gulls, and one persistent youngster in its baby brown plumage, trying to persuade its mother it still needed food. It followed her everywhere, cheeping pitifully, until she lost her temper and chased it away, her beak stabbing relentlessly. The young bird began to turn the weed over, looking for food, but it was not yet experienced, and Paddy Joe saw it pecking busily at a polythene bottle that had been cast up by the tide. He thought it remarkably stupid.

Storm had found himself a new occupation. He had watched Tomkin and Paddy Joe collect driftwood for the fires, and he busied himself bringing pieces of wood to Paddy Joe, his tail waving happily, proud of himself for helping. Soon there was a pile of it at the edge of the beach, and Paddy Joe began to carry it back to the cottage and put it in the outhouse beside the peats, ready for use. Storm added his piece at every journey. By the time Tomkin returned there was enough fuel to last a week.

Tomkin had caught seven fish; two codlings, a haddock, two sea bream, and two large plaice. He had tried fishing at all depths. There was enough to share with Mac and Andy when they came for Paddy Joe. The Colonel, arriving empty-handed, poured himself a whisky and soda and warmed himself by the fire. It had turned chill with evening, and he had been standing thigh deep all day in ice-cold water which was running off the mountain.

Paddy Joe ate fried fish and chips until he wondered if he would have room for the baked custard that Tomkin had made to follow. Tomkin had no doubt and served a huge portion.

'You'll find it cold tonight,' he said. 'Stoke up. A full belly makes a warm man. They always told us that in the army.'

'Along with the information that an army marches on its stomach,' the Colonel said, and everyone laughed.

Mac and Andy came soon after the first owl had hooted her welcome to the dusk. Mac looked at Paddy Joe and grinned.

'The wind is kind tonight,' he said, in his soft Scots voice. 'The beasties will not scent us if we take good care.'

Paddy Joe followed the two men up the hill beyond

the cottage garden wall. Storm moved close at heel, as silent as his shadow, used to their night-time prowls with Tomkin. Tonight Tomkin and the Colonel had gone fishing in the loch. Looking back, Paddy Joe saw the dinghy, outlined by brilliance. The dipped oars dripped with sparkles of light. The wake creamed behind, glittering. Arrowed fish sparked the water. Everything was alive with phosphorescence. Tomkin had told him it was caused by a minute creature quite invisible to the human eye, but he had never seen the effect before. The loch was a miracle of enchantment, unbelievably beautiful under the cold moon.

An owl flew low, hooting mournfully. Storm stiffened and his cold nose butted Paddy Joe's knee. Mac signalled with his hand. A wildcat was walking, queen-like, down the glade towards them. Moonlight shone full on her thick, sleek, striped coat, and bushy ringed tail, and her small neat face. She heard a sound, turned her head so that her eyes gleamed briefly, and then she was gone, and the glade was empty and the hooting owl flew over again, mourning the lack of food.

The four of them crouched under the trees, as still as the bright stars that shone from a clear sky. Storm was as motionless as any rock. There was a rustling on the hill as a big animal, unafraid, bulldozed through the undergrowth towards them.

Paddy Joe saw the badger first. It was the boar, coming away from its sett, sniffing the air, striped muzzle lifted high, white bands conspicuous in the moonlight. He was very wary.

Paddy Joe's leg itched, and an insect crawled over his face. It was almost impossible to keep still, but he knew that if he moved the badger would vanish as surely as had the wildcat. He concentrated on the entrance of the sett, and was rewarded by seeing the sow peer out cautiously, and then climb from the opening, and sit to scratch heartily, her hind leg thumping the ground. Storm was taut with excitement, longing to move, but knew he should stay. Paddy Joe kept a tight hold of the Alsatian's collar, just in case.

The cubs wanted to play. They ran behind the sow, tiny agile bears, pushing against each other in their eagerness. The boar walked over to his earth pit, dug far away from the sett so that the ground nearby and inside it should not be fouled. On his way he caught an alien whiff, and after he had visited the pit he came back and began to scout around.

The watchers froze, hardly breathing, as the female, leaving father to guard the young, began to bring out the bedding. She dragged it right away from the sett and started to take in fresh, gathering leaves and ferns from the clearing.

The cubs rolled together, puppy like, spitting softly, snarling at one another with an odd low sound, and then chased each other like school-children playing tig.

The boar found a mole and killed it. He shared it with the cubs, who were still shy of him. They had spent their first weeks alone with their mother, and only recently met the father. He was grubbing for beetles, rooting them out to give first to one cub and then another. The cubs, watching him, began to copy his actions, and gained confidence, so that one of them snatched food from his jaws and backed in surprise when he growled, warning the small beast away.

The boar was bothered. He sniffed the air uneasily, lifting his head. Paddy Joe was sure they could not be scented, as they were downwind of the animal, but something worried the beast. He began to root in the undergrowth. A moment later, he circled warily. He snarled at the sow, who had come to find him, and she, sensing his unease, shepherded the cubs into the sett, snapping in fury at their heels when they lagged,

43

unwilling to leave the excitement of night and wind and moonshine.

The badger rolled. There was a sharp snap, and he stood, shaking his head angrily. He lumbered away, and vanished. Mac waited until the rustling in the undergrowth ceased, and went to look in the bracken. Someone had set a spring trap. Mac looked at it. He hated the things. Paddy Joe and Andy, standing behind him, saw that the old boar had flung his entire weight on the snare, and sprung it, harmlessly. Satisfied, the boar had ambled away. There was no danger to his family. Mac collected the snare and, later, put it in the car, to take it away and ensure it was not laid again.

They saw nothing more that night. Dawn came, grey, with a sly wind and a thin rain, and Paddy Joe followed Mac and Andy to the beach, where they helped the Colonel and Tomkin unload the fish they had caught in the night. Tomkin kept enough for breakfast and gave the rest to Mac and Andy to sell, or to exchange for food or for shot for the shotguns. It had been a good night's fishing.

Mac and Andy knew many tales about the island and Paddy Joe was fascinated as he listened.

'I mind the last tenants, Mistress Campbell, and her husband Ian,' said Andy thoughtfully. 'It was a sad story, for Ian was a great smuggler, and he brought all kinds of contraband to the island. He hid it in the cave beyond the jetty. There is no cave now, as the cliff has fallen and the entrance is closed with rocks. One night he set to sea to meet a Frenchman who was bringing brandy. The story goes that there was a great gale that night, one of the worst ever known, and Ian Campbell and his boat vanished and were never seen again. His widow mourned him and became strange in her grief and as odd in her way as the Hermit before her. Some said that his daughter Morag and her fisherman had escaped the seas and settled on the mainland, and that Mistress Meg Campbell was the Hermit's grand-daughter, but no one ever knew the right of that. The Big House had been built by then, and the laird allowed her to stay on the island in the little cottage on the hill. It is now in ruins. The land agent and his family had your cottage then. It was more convenient. Then the land agent left and the laird died, and Mistress Campbell came to live in the cottage, as her own was tumbling down.'

Paddy Joe could have listened to the soft Scots voice for ever.

'Aye,' Mac said. 'Mistress Campbell, like Morag, had her way with the beasts. She had two wildcat kittens, and some said they knew her, and came when she called, though they were never house cats. And she adopted a collie which belonged to an old shepherd who died. The dog vanished one stormy night and no one ever knew what happened to it. You want to watch your dog, lad. There's strange things happen on the island. She never spoke to people after that, but she spoke to the beasts, and the badgers knew her voice, and deer and pheasants fed from her hands. There were some in the village said she was a witch, but I think she was a lonely woman, and she found greater kindness from the wild creatures about her than she found from her own kind.'

'She knew more about the wild things than many a man today, so they say,' Andy went on.

'She could draw, too,' Mac said. 'Sheena McDougal at the garage remembers her sitting on the sea wall drawing the birds. She was a fierce old woman. I mind her myself; I once came to the island with my shotgun and she chased me away with stones, and took the gun when I dropped it and unloaded it and smashed the stock with a stone. She flung it after me, calling out that I'd no' shoot beast or bird on her island. I was only a

45

wee lad, not as old as you are now, Paddy Joe, and I ran for dear life, and it was a long day before I dared come back. I mind her voice now. It was high and harsh, like a seabird crying, and I dreamed of it at night.'

Paddy Joe slept in the tent again that night. He went to bed early, unable to keep awake after so long with Mac and Andy. Tomorrow he and Storm would explore alone. Who knew what they might see?

6

Paddy Joe woke next day to a wind that screamed through the trees, tossing them aside as if they were slender saplings and not sturdy well-grown trunks that had weathered centuries. It was dawn. A grey light had come to the world, and Storm was lying beside him, nose sniffing the air, ears erect.

Paddy Joe crawled out of his sleeping bag. The wind was cold. He dragged jeans and jersey over his pyjamas, smoothed his hand through his tousled hair, and was ready for the day. The cottage curtains were still drawn across the windows. Neither the Colonel nor Tomkin was awake.

The birds were greeting the first faint light, and the woods were noisy, chatter and twitter and caw added to the sound of the wind. Excitement rode high, whenever the wind blew hard. Even Paddy Joe was affected by it. He wanted to run and dance and shout and romp with his dog. He wanted to see what else was astir and what creatures came to the nearby spring to drink.

He quieted Storm with a hand against the dog's neck. Storm resisted, but Tomkin had taught him well and at last he obeyed. Tomkin, during the war, had trained Alsatians for guard duty, and for messenger duty, and knew as much as any man about dogs. Not everything, he always said. You never stop learning. There's always something new to find out, about the way a dog works, or tries to think, or some new peculiarity of his behaviour. Watch your dog, Tomkin always said. Those ears will tell you things you never dreamed of. Paddy Joe looked at Storm now. The dog had frozen, one paw lifted, head cocked, ears pointing to the thicket in front of them. Side by side boy and dog waited, breathless. Paddy Joe knew the wind was blowing in his face, so that whatever lay hidden in the bushes was unable to smell either of them. Their scent was blown behind them. The leaves parted, and out of the shadows cast by the trees stepped a roe deer and her two kids. They were twins, so like one another that no one could tell them apart. They came boldly into the clearing and began to play, chasing after one another, round and round in mazy excited circles, first one leading and then the other, while the mother grazed, and lifted her head to sniff the air, and bent to feed again.

Behind Paddy Joe, the buck barked. The doe looked towards him, saw boy and dog, and bleated to her young. They ran to her and in a moment had merged into the undergrowth. The light was brighter. There was a hint of sun shining on mist that drifted over the grass. Paddy Joe pushed Storm to the ground and shook a finger at him. The Alsatian knew that this meant 'down' and 'stay'. It was useful to teach the dog to obey hand signals as well as words, then silence need not be broken and Paddy Joe often watched animals in the woods. He had never watched in such a place before.

He might have been alone in the wilds, miles from civilisation. The trees surrounded him, the noise of the wind increasing minute by minute. Behind the wind was the roar of the sea as angry waves crashed on the beaches; he heard the suck and swirl and surge of water on the shingle, and the cry of the gulls as they wheeled and screamed, maddened by the gale.

Paddy Joe climbed a small tree and settled himself in

the crook of its branches. It swayed in the breeze so that he felt as if he were high on the mast of a ship at sea, rocking as the boat rocked. From his perch he could see down the path to the beach, and also see a rocky outcrop that poked into the water. He watched for movement. Birds hunted in the undergrowth for insects. A rabbit, intent, ran across the small clearing, its ears alert for danger. It stopped, sitting on its hind legs, looking about it, nose sniffing, forepaws close against its chest.

It caught the scent of dog and in a second was off, white scut bobbing, and the flash of movement was more than the dog could bear. All lessons were forgotten. Nothing existed but the bounding tail in front of him, and Paddy Joe called in vain as rabbit and dog vanished from the clearing.

Paddy Joe slid down the tree and ran after them, whistling. Storm was blind to everything but the animal in front of him. He was deaf to all shouts. His nose was filled with rabbit scent. His mouth lolled open, panting with excitement. The rabbit slipped between the trees, and fled, headlong, bobtail bouncing, until it came to a hole in the little wall that bordered the beach. It was through and along the ditch and into the bank, and Storm was left digging frantically, earth flying high, tail wagging furiously.

Paddy Joe was angry when he found the dog. He was angry with himself. Tomkin had warned him, over and over again. Dogs have short memories. They don't stay trained. You have to remind them. Don't neglect those lessons, Paddy Joe. Storm had been totally obedient, and now he was not. He needed teaching all over again.

Paddy Joe walked towards the dog. He spoke sharply, as Storm came towards him, tail waving.

'Bad dog!'

The Alsatian's tail drooped. He hated scolding. There had been little need before. And Paddy Joe had done the wrong thing again, as the dog thought he was being rebuked for coming back to his master. Paddy Joe looped his handkerchief through the dog's collar, and walked through the woods. The day had been spoiled. Storm, pulling against restraint, longing to run, was no longer completely reliable, or under control. Paddy Joe hated the island, and its temptations; hated the Colonel and Tomkin, who did not understand how it felt to be a boy; he wanted his grandmother back again. Grandee would have understood. And she would have reminded Paddy Joe to give the dog his daily lesson. She would never have expected him to remember by himself. She always reminded him.

The trees throbbed in the wind. The woods were eerie, and Paddy Joe could believe in goblins, ghosts, and witch folk, living out of sight of people, hidden among the trees. Behind the wind was a wild keening, an echo that might be Morag, singing to the seals. It was easy to imagine clawed creatures riding the wind, fierce and angry, hurling themselves among the tossing branches.

Storm lifted his head and growled, deep in his throat, an angry rumble. Paddy Joe quieted the dog, as a tabby cat prowled towards them, along the path. The wind hid their scent and carried no message. Small-faced and dainty, she lifted her head and Paddy Joe thought how pretty she was. Then he noticed the big bushy tail and saw how she turned suddenly at a leaf that fell behind her, and spat wickedly, fluffing her fur to make her seem twice her nomal size. Her back was arched, a ridge showing along her spine, and her ring-striped tail was rigid. He knew that this was no tame puss, but the wild-cat, hellion of the woods, the tiger of the forests and the Scottish moors.

There was a sudden noise in the trees, a honk echoing high above the wind, and Paddy Joe jumped and slipped with a flurry of sound that made Storm bark angrily, sure that they were being attacked. The wildcat vanished, and an enraged and frightened cock pheasant that had seen her as she walked across the clearing, and called his horror, stopped to preen his handsome feathers and soothe his feelings now that she had gone.

There was a ghost presence, as the wildcat showed herself briefly among the bushes. Paddy Joe saw her again, a moving pattern in a dapple of light and shade, blending with the foliage, unreal. Her strong legs carried her lightly through thorn and bramble, until she was hidden from sight.

It must be breakfast time. He was starving and dawn was a memory. The sun was bright. He walked back through the windlashed wood, Storm pacing sedately at heel. The vixen raced across his path, a dashing creature, her thick brush waving. She turned her head to look at him. Storm prickled with excitement and Paddy Joe grabbed his collar, not at all sure that the dog could be trusted not to chase after the fox. Storm was becoming very disobedient indeed. They climbed over the wall, and walked along the shore, watching the sea.

A yodel summoned him to eat. Tomkin was standing at the edge of the beach, waving, and Paddy Joe picked his way over the rocks, disturbing a crab that stood on tiptoe and brandished its nippers at him. Storm stared in amazement and Paddy Joe grinned, thinking how brave the crab must be to defy two giants, towering above it.

'Anyone'd think you weren't hungry,' Tomkin said, as Paddy Joe ran up to him. 'I found a hen living wild in the garden, so we've eggs for breakfast as well as smoked mackerel. And fresh raspberries. I've been busy, even if there's some as hasn't.' Paddy Joe grinned. The Colonel was already eating, his mind more on salmon than on Paddy Joe.

'I saw a wildcat today, and a vixen,' Paddy Joe said. 'I'd like pictures of them.'

'Maybe we can use the Colonel's camera,' Tomkin said. He frowned, trying to remember something. 'I know, Paddy Joe. You remember Storm was trying to tell us something the other night after supper? He kept pawing at our legs, and sniffing?'

Paddy Joe nodded.

'I bet he smelled the vixen or the wildcat. If we watch him, he'll lead us to them.'

'Can we go today?' asked Paddy Joe.

'Tomkin shook his head,

'Too blustery. We might not be able to get right side of the wind, and it's going to change with the tide and blow fitful. That'd give us away. We'll have to wait for the right weather, or we'll just waste our time. What about a swim when we've done these spuds? I'll show you how to improve that crawl. We can swim in the big pool left by the tide. It's much too rough to risk the sea today.'

Paddy Joe settled down to wait. He had promised never to swim alone in either river or sea. It was too easy to get into trouble, and when alone there was no one to help out. Rivers had deep holes in places, and thick weeds in others, where even an expert swimmer could get trapped and be unable to free himself. At sea, there were swift currents off shore, and here, when the tide was receding, there was a current which even Tomkin could not fight. It was necessary to wait for the flooding tide, and to watch that the water did not get too deep. They dared not swim beyond the curve of rock where the current flowed round the island, grabbing everything and everyone that came into its hold. Luckily there was a large pool, deep enough for swimming, left by the outgoing tide, so that they could bathe most days. Paddy Joe waited, and thought that Tomkin would never finish the jobs about the house. Storm was restless too, eager to run and hunt in the woods and on the beaches. Paddy Joe was sure he would explode with impatience long before Tomkin was ready.

7

Storm paced the beach while Paddy Joe and Tomkin were swimming. He was bored and wanted to run and play. He nosed the rocks, but the smells did not attract him, and the tang of seaweed irritated his nostrils. He wandered to the edge of the sea and barked, and Tomkin called him to be quiet, and went on showing Paddy Joe how to perfect his crawl.

The waves out in the loch were enormous and even in the pool there was a ruffle on the water and white caps tossed by the wind. It was cool, and Tomkin had his eye on the incoming tide. As soon as the sea reached the pool there would be danger and a quick flooding and it would be time to get ashore. He forgot to watch the dog and Paddy Joe forgot everything in his desire to swim better.

There was a tang on the wind. Animal tang. Fox tang. Musk tang hanging on the air, strong enough for a man to smell and a thousand times stronger to a dog. It was an invitation to hunt. It was heart racing, breath quickening, so that Storm lifted his head and sniffed, the smell coming from the wood behind him, airborne, breast high, total enchantment, something no dog could resist.

There was no one to see him go. No one to call as he left the beach and put his nose down to the trail the fox had left in the wood. The scent was everywhere, was all around him, was teasing on the wind, calling him to follow. Nothing existed but the pleasure of the moment.

Paddy Joe was forgotten. Storm was a wild dog again, every vestige of training vanished. He left the beach and climbed the bank, and was hidden among the trees, and neither Tomkin nor Paddy Joe realised that the dog had gone until they clambered out of the water.

'Storm!' Paddy Joe shouted.

Only the echoes answered. The wind was roaring, bull-like, through the woods, and the sky was darker than before. It was cold, and a chill fear made Paddy Joe even colder.

'He can't be far,' Tomkin said, and whistled.

There was no reply. Paddy Joe watched for the familiar bounding shape of the Alsatian. There was nothing—nothing but the trees, angered by the wind. The sea raged and flung driftwood on to the beach. Paddy Joe stared at the waves. Surely Storm had not gone swimming? He wished he had not forgotten the dog. He dressed quietly, desperately anxious.

'He's gone hunting,' Tomkin said, 'Let's follow the trail. The island's too small for him to go far.'

It was small, but it held many dangers. The waves pounding on the rocks, the overhang near the jetty, the cave on the other side of the island, all spelled trouble. Suppose Storm met the wildcat and she attacked him? Could he stand against her wickedness? Could he fight against those armoured paws, and needle-like teeth? Suppose he was caught in a snare, like the one the old badger had sprung? The dog know nothing about snares.

'Storm!'

'Storm!'

'Storm!'

It sounded as if they were shouting to the gale, and only the gale answered. They rounded the curve of the island. Nothing moved on the marsh, nothing walked near the wood. Grey sea met grey sky. Grey rocks lay on the beach. There was no track nor trace nor hint nor sign of the dog along the path.

They searched the beach. They searched the cottage. They searched the outhouses and the ruins on the hill and the empty rooms of the deserted mansion where only the swallows lived, and nothing moved but torn paper blown across the dusty floors.

Paddy Joe did not want his supper, but Tomkin cooked an omelette and refused to clear away until the boy had eaten every mouthful. The Colonel was still fishing. They left the dishes steeping in the sink, and climbed the hill. The wind was a hurricane, yelling among the trees, hurtling out of the sky, chasing leaf and twig and tugging hair and clothing. The wind was an enemy, filled with hatred. The wind was torment, threatening safety. Far away, a branch split from a tree with a crescendo of sound, and Tomkin called the search off, lest they were killed by a falling trunk.

Paddy Joe could not settle to anything. If Storm were not trapped by the tide, or imprisoned somewhere, he would have come home. Something had happened to him. Suppose there had been another snare in the woods? Suppose he were lying in pain, caught by his leg, unable to free himself? Suppose he were dead?

8

The Colonel came home and listened in silence. There
was nothing to be said and it was too late for recrimina-
tions. Bed was unthinkable. Paddy Joe would never be
able to sleep. He could not face the dark stairway or the
silent room. He was conscious of the wind in the trees, of
the steady drip of rain, of the crackle of wood in the
hearth. He was aware of Tomkin's silence, and the
glances he and the Colonel exchanged, and of his own
restlessness so that he prowled from door to window,
looked into the garden, and called, trying to shout above
the din of wind and waves. He watched forlornly for the
shape of the dog, running through the bushes, eyes
eager, tail waving. There was nothing outside but the
windy dark.

'Nothing to be done till morning,' Tomkin said. He
was annoyed about the dog, and worried, and sorry for
Paddy Joe. 'He'll be all right. He's a sensible animal.'
He had been a well-trained dog till Paddy Joe forgot to
give him his lessons. It was much too late to remedy
matters now. If Storm had remembered his training he
would have stayed on the beach till they came. Nothing
would have moved him; not fox, or stoat, or rabbit or
wildcat. Paddy Joe looked into the darkness. Why had
he forgotten? Why had he stopped bothering? Why had
he let his dog relapse into disobedience? He had no
answer. It had been easier not to bother. Tomkin should

have made him remember. Tomkin knew what it was like to be a boy and have so many interesting things to do that you forgot some of the duller ones. It had been fine when he had started training, but somehow the novelty had worn off and he had taken the dog's obedience for granted. He should have listened to Tomkin.

'No use wearing yourself out with fretting,' Tomkin said, as Paddy Joe walked over to the window for the hundredth time. 'Did I ever tell you of the night I was out with a drunken donkey?'

Paddy Joe shook his head. He was not very interested in drunken donkeys. He peered out among the trees, thinking he had seen a movement, but whatever had been there was gone, or else it was a trick of the lighting. The hurricane lamps cast weird shadows.

Tomkin did not answer immediately. He was trying to master his tongue. He wanted to upbraid Paddy Joe, tell him it was his own fault, and now he was suffering for his own laziness. It was pointless to rub it in. The boy was desperate enough, already. Tomkin poured boiling water out of the kettle into the teapot and then poured tea for the three of them. The Colonel was sitting quietly, smoking his pipe. He had been out in the dark, calling the dog, and had given up reluctantly. His eyes too strayed frequently to the window. It was a wild night. Paddy Joe thought of his dog, outside, alone, in the wind and the rain. Worry needled him again and he felt sick.

'We were out on patrol in the desert,' Tomkin said. 'Back in the war, that was. Hot, windy, sand in your teeth and your hair and your clothes, and warm water that tasted of sand to drink from your water bottles. Never went anywhere without them. If you did, you were a goner.'

He stopped to drink his tea, and Paddy Joe waited impatiently, his thoughts on the missing dog, rather than on Tomkin's story.

'There were six of us. We knew there was a German outpost near, so we left four of us with the donkey that carried our supplies, and two of us scouted around. The Germans began to fire at us, and we fired back, and chased them off. They retreated, and when we went up to their camp, we found nothing there but a big barrel of wine they must have pinched from some village. The barrel was full, and when we took out the bung, it was a rough red wine, but it tasted good. We loaded it on to the donkey.'

'Go on,' said Paddy Joe, sure he knew what was to come. The donkey would knock out the bung in the night. He was wrong.

'We ran into another patrol on the way back. Or maybe it was the same one. We took shelter in some dunes, and exchanged shots for a time. At last the Germans withdrew; I think there were more of us than of them. No one was hurt, and our barrel of wine was OK so back we went to camp.'

Paddy Joe could see the small procession of tired men, watching the desert for signs of the enemy, walking slowly in the blazing heat of a tropical sun, dusty but content, with the donkey beside them and a barrel of wine as their reward when at last they reached their base.

'We got back and unloaded that cask,' Tomkin said. 'It was lighter than a handful of sand! Just a small amount of wine swilling round in the bottom. The Germans had shot a bullet in one side and out the other, just three inches up; and every drop of wine had spilled. We unsaddled the donkey and discovered his fur was soaked with wine. We hadn't the water to wash him. He spent the night trying to lick himself clean, and you should have seen the poor beast in the morning! He couldn't walk straight, and could only just stand. We had to give him four days to recover. Poor old Mutt; he was a sight.'

Tomkin laughed.

'We all laughed at him, but it wasn't really funny. I felt proper mean about it, but who'd have thought that out of all that shooting, one'd go straight through the barrel.'

'It's as well it wasn't lower, or it'd have gone straight through the donkey,' the Colonel said.

It was no good. Paddy Joe had only half heard the story and could think of nothing but his dog. He must do something active. He could not sit still. He went out into the hall and looked at the big cupboard under the stairs. It was full of the junk of years and he wondered what was inside. He opened the door, and then went to the kitchen to fetch the big torch that Tomkin kept for emergencies. It was odd to be there alone. He almost expected Storm to come and find out what he was doing. But there was no dog.

The cupboard was enormous. Paddy Joe moved a pile of old newspapers. A mouse had made herself a nest inside the papers. She had chewed the central part to pulp and hollowed out a cavity in which she lay with five almost hairless, blind babies, so tiny that Paddy Joe couldn't believe in them. He looked at the minute claws, and the miniature bodies, and the little mouths suckling at their mother. She stared at him, terrified.

The bulk of the paper was solid. Paddy Joe lifted it and took the nest to show to Tomkin. He peered down at the mouse.

'She's a long-tailed field mouse, not a house mouse,' he said. 'She must have come in for warmth. Put the pile of papers in the outhouse, Paddy Joe. She doesn't do much harm in a place like this.'

Paddy Joe took the nest outside. The outhouse was attached to the kitchen, and full of intriguing things. There was a blacksmith's anvil and an enormous axe that reminded him of a headman's axe; a scythe, rusty with disuse; part of a harrow, left by some farmer years ago. It was not as intriguing as the cupboard under the stairs, and he went back to explore.

There were broken chairs, covered in dust; a broom, and a witch's broom, used for sweeping up leaves. And there was a box, a large metal cash box. Paddy Joe opened it. It was full of yellowed papers. He took it back to the living-room.

'Who lives here now?' Paddy Joe asked.

'No one,' the Colonel said. 'It's let in summer to people like us and in winter it stands empty. The last tenant died about ten years ago, and the owner finds it more profitable to let it to fishermen and birdwatchers than to rent it all through the year. He couldn't charge nearly as much.'

'Then whose are these?' Paddy Joe asked.

The Colonel leaned forward curiously.

'Letters,' Paddy Joe said. He separated one sheet from the others. 'It's got a date on it . . . it isn't a letter. It's a sort of diary. It's all about a farm, and about the animals here. Look!'

The Colonel picked up one of the pages. It was brittle and dry, stained with age, and the spidery writing was difficult to decipher. He began to read slowly.

May 14*th* 1872. It is, as ever, lonely here. I often think of the Black Hermit, who once owned this cottage, and of his daughter, Morag. It is easy to believe they haunt this place, when the wind runs wild in the trees, and the wildcats scream, and the vixen calls her mate. Sometimes I think I will die of being alone, while my man is fishing. I listen with terror in my heart, knowing the sea to be wicked, and remorseless; merciless to those who make mistakes. Yet Ian would never leave the sea. Even when he is with me, he is always listening for the sound of the waves and watching the weather signs in the sky, so that he can leave on the tide. I wish I had a child to keep me company, but that is not to be. Both my babies died and they tell me I can have no more. Ian has brought me a dog. A beautiful collie with sorrowful eyes. His master died and he is fretting for him. I hope he will soon settle. I need his company. Tonight we dare not walk outside. The wind is wild, and on such a night as this the young girl whom the Black Hermit wed was killed by a falling tree and left him lonely. If only Ian would come home, and learn to farm our beasts. The land is so hard and there is such poor grazing. I have to beg hay from the MacDonalds for my Nettie and her calf. And the little bull calf is so thin that I doubt if I will ever sell him.'

'It's a diary,' the Colonel said. 'I wonder who she was, living here alone. It must have been frightening for a woman by herself.'

'Especially on a night like this,' Tomkin said. 'The wind's dropped, but listen to that sea. Imagine being out in a boat.'

The roar of the water on the beach drowned all other sounds. Paddy Joe looked at the papers.

'My dog has vanished. I have searched the island for him. I pray he is not dead. It is desolate without him. I cannot look now until daybreak. It is too dangerous in the dark. I hope he has not gone to seek his old master.'

Paddy Joe's heart was an enormous ache inside him. Tears pricked his eyes and there was a stone in his throat. He swallowed. It was unbearable.

'I'll go over in the morning to see our landlord and ask if we can read through it, and if he knows who lived here then.' The Colonel was anxious to distract Paddy Joe. '1872. Victoria was Queen; the British Empire was coming to the height of its power; England was made up of the incredibly rich and the unbelievably poor; nobody ever dreamed that man would set foot on the moon. It's a world that we'd find hard to believe in, Paddy Joe, but perhaps if we read the diary, we'll learn a lot more than we think.'

He put the papers away in the box and stood it carefully on the bookcase. Paddy Joe looked at the books, but they were very dull; a medical dictionary, a railway timetable for 1922; and a number of old histories of big houses in Scotland. The pages were fusty and the print too tiny to read with any comfort.

'Bed,' Tomkin said. 'It's after midnight, lad, and we need to be fresh for the morning. Ten to one we'll find the dog sitting on the doorstep, waiting for us to wake.'

Tomkin meant to be kind, but Paddy Joe did not believe him. He took the torch, and climbed the stairs to his room, watching shadows that were thick with menace, threaten him from beyond the corners of the heavy old-fashioned furniture. It must have been creepy, living before electric light, when no one could banish the midnight terrors with a flick of the fingers. Paddy Joe had never appreciated civilisation before. He wanted to call to Tomkin to come upstairs with him, but that would have been babyish.

He undressed and crawled into bed. The sheets were cold and the lumpy mattress offered little comfort. Last night his dog had slept beside him. Last night both had been safe, and the wind had only whispered around the tent. Last night he had thought that the life he knew would go on for ever, always the same, with Storm there beside him.

Paddy Joe lay with his eyes open, staring at the unfriendly dark. The wind was easing, and a glimmer of moonlight shone through ragged clouds, lighting the corner of the room so that it seemed to Paddy Joe that a woman stood there, watching him, her eyes sad. He slept, but his dreams were troubled, and a girl ran through the woods, calling, calling, calling to a dog. Then the girl vanished and an older woman, thin, with a wistful face, bent over Paddy Joe, and he stared up at her, knowing he was dreaming, yet not quite sure, and she looked down at him, and took his hand.

A moment later they were on the beach, walking over

the rocks, taking the same path as the girl, and Storm was beyond him, swimming in the sea, swimming away from him, out of his sight, only his head visible. The waves grew, and the dog's head disappeared, and Paddy Joe felt a lump in his throat. He turned to look at the woman, who was staring out to sea.

'My dog has gone to look for his master,' she said. 'His master was old, and he died, and Glenn will not settle with me.'

Her voice was blown away on the wind. Paddy Joe woke to find his pillow soaked with tears. He woke to find day had banished nightmare, and brought a dull grey morning to the world. He went down to find Tomkin had already prepared breakfast and the Colonel had eaten his and was about to go out. Paddy Joe opened the door and called, but no dog answered. Nightmare returned, but now he was fully awake.

'I'll look on the north side of the island, towards the jetty,' the Colonel said. 'I don't suppose the dog's gone far.'

Paddy Joe did not want to eat, but he forced himself to swallow. He could taste nothing. He remembered his dream, and the woman watching the dog's head vanish under the waves. He shivered.

'We'll find him, lad,' the Colonel said. The door slammed behind the old man, and the wind whispered over the bushes.

'She didn't find Glenn,' Paddy Joe said. Tomkin stared at him, wondering what had got into the boy's head now, and neither he nor Paddy Joe remembered that the dog's name had never been mentioned in the diary, and Tomkin did not question how he knew.

9

The clouds vanished. The sun, as if to make up for the rain, blazed from a cloudless sky, dazzling on the water. Tomkin, looking for wood for the kitchen fire, heard the corncrake again, and wondered if he could find where it nested. The young would be grown by now, but the nest might still lie in the thick grass, in a hollow. Tomkin had jobs he must do, so Paddy Joe went out by himself to look for Storm, promising to be careful. Only it was difficult to remember his promise. He wanted his dog found. He needed his dog desperately. Storm, Storm, Storm. He called until his voice was no more than a harsh whimper. Storm! No movement anywhere.

He climbed a tall tree on the wooded hill above the cottage, and looked about him. The island was so very small. A spit of land fingered into the loch at the landward end. On the far coast the sea thundered on a rocky beach; here the loch was narrow, the other side of it only a few hundred yards away. It widened again, and lay in a long bay which in its turn opened to the sea. Not a tail waved. Not an ear flickered. Nothing moved.

Across the loch the mountains rose in rolling ranges on the mainland, changing shape as shadows raced across them; now near, now far; now blue; now purple; now welcoming; now forbidding. The light changed as the clouds gathered above the hills, and each flicker revealed new hollows and peaks, so that the landscape was never the same for even ten seconds. The mountains sheltered the island from the severity of the gales, deflecting rain showers that helped the climate, so that here grew many flowers unique to that part of Scotland.

When the tide rose high under the causeway, the blue water lapped on every shore. At low tide the bare bones of the island showed, and, if the water went out far enough, ribbed sand lay at the edge of the rocks, pooled with water, and it was possible to cross dry shod to the mainland. Herons fished, gulls haunted the pools, hoping for flotsam, and the bright orange weed lay everywhere, patching grey rock and fine white sand.

Paddy Joe noted the shape of the island, and determined to explore every inch and search everywhere, when he had found Storm. He looked for movement again but there was none. He climbed down the tree and walked quietly. The ground was spongy with bogmoss. Once he paused to look curiously at a small clump of orchids. He marked their position, wondering what they were. Orchids seemed to grow quite freely here. He had never seen any in England.

He came to the top of Seal Rock, and stopped. The wildcat was on the beach beside one of the small pools, her head, prick-eared, on one side, as she waited. Perhaps Storm was near, and would scent her, and come running, out of the woods, ears erect, tail eager. Paddy Joe held his breath, hoping. The wildcat loved fish. She did not understand the movement of the sea, which often chased her up the beach, but she learned to watch it, knowing that when it went away, leaving ridged rocks holding deep, still pools, she could safely walk there, and hunt for food. She crouched over a pool in which were fronded anemones. There were many kinds. Paddy Joe had seen them two days before; some were small dark brown globules, close against the rock; others, golden, or blue with red spots, or strawberry coloured, waved fragile flowery fronds as they clung beneath rocky ledges. The little cat had once put out an interested paw to tap these tantalising waving beauties, and withdrawn it hurriedly, licking fiercely in an attempt to neutralise the myriad sharp stings that made her paw throb and tingle. After that she left them alone.

Paddy Joe watched her as she sat on the warm rocks, delighting in sunshine that bathed her fur, and reflected back at her from the hard granite surface. Her bushy tail waved gently as she gazed, wide-eyed, into the water. Paddy Joe watched the woods behind. Surely Storm would come. He could never resist the scent of cat. Paddy Joe knew the dog always wanted to chase any that they met.

Seaweed masked the depths, but the cat waited quietly and soon her patience was rewarded as a silvery shape darted momentarily into the sunshine and flicked a derisory tail before diving into safety among the weeds.

The cat began to purr. She loved fishing. Ears flattened, she poised herself over the pool, one paw hanging loosely over the rocky edge. A movement from the water. Sweep of claw and flash of silver and the fish was on the rock beside her.

As it lay, gills widening and shutting as it gasped, small mouth gaping, the cat patted the flailing tail. She spent a few moments amusing herself as the fish twisted and jumped, trying to find its way back into the water. The need for food was too big to master. She bit deep, killing, and crouched low, pausing to swear at gulls that arrowed through the air above her head, hoping to drive her off her catch and find themselves an easy dinner.

No dog appeared.

Paddy Joe left her, and crept into the wood which bordered the beach. No one had cultivated here for a long time. Trees grew thickly, their trunks thin and slender as they fought one another for food from the ground and light from the sun. The undergrowth was dense, matted and tangled, and it was hard to find a way through. Wherever there was a clearing under the trees, there was bog, spongy under his feet. He stopped for a moment to watch a young squirrel hunt along the ground for fallen acorns. The little beast raced up a tree and looked down at him, chattering angrily. He ran along the branch again, a small fluffy creature, his tail ratlike, the thick fur only half grown. He disappeared into a hole in the trunk. Storm would have been hard to hold, impatient to hunt, had he been there. Paddy Joe swallowed the ache in his throat but the pain did not go.

Paddy Joe quartered the wood. He hunted through the trees, and under the bushes. He called until he was hoarse. He chased after a fleeting shadow. It was cast by a cloud flying beneath the sun. He followed the sound of heavy rustling. A bird was turning over dry dead leaves in search of insects. He pushed his hand down a large fox-hole, and lay flat and tried to see into the darkness. There was nothing but silence and the stink of fox and decaying food. The fox had caught a young bird and eaten half and left the rest behind. There were feathers lying all round the opening in the ground.

The dark trees arched under the sky. It was ghostly in the wood, a place of haunting shadows, where every sound was suspect. Paddy Joe had forgotten what it was like to walk without his dog. For more than three years they had been constant companions. He started at every sound, and looked about for Storm, unable to believe that the dog had really vanished. The guilt of the day before rose to irritate him. It was his own fault. Please, God, let me find Storm and I won't forget again. Not ever.

There was a movement at the edge of the ride, and Paddy Joe caught his breath. Surely that was a dog's ear outlined against the sky. Paddy Joe went to investigate.

The wind had teased a spiky twig. There was only a slender tree with a small bush beside it. Yet he had seen so clearly. He began to lose all hope. The shadows gave way to bright sunlight and he blinked at the dazzle. He was beside the only stream on the island, a small runnel that was too small for the colonel to fish. It fed the well from which they drew their water. Beyond it there was a tree, dragged from the earth, its roots reaching towards the sky. Paddy Joe thought of the tree that had killed Morag's mother and wondered where it had fallen. He could hear a jay screeching, alarm in its voice. The call was picked up by a chaffinch, echoed in the chitter of an angry starling, and added to by the sharp sawing note of a heron from a nearby tree.

Something large and heavy was running down the clearing towards the beach. Paddy Joe turned to look, delight in his face. He called, sharp and clear, his voice triumphant.

'Storm, here then, good dog. Come!'

The animal broke out of the wood, and turned to face the boy. Paddy Joe's elation died, as the stag caught his scent and trotted along the margin of the wood until he came to a gap in the trees, and vanished among the mossy trunks.

It was nearly lunchtime. There was no room for anything but sorrow. He would never be able to eat. He walked slowly home, his feet dragging. The Colonel was there before him, drinking his soup. He nodded at Paddy Joe. Words were useless now. Tomkin was in the kitchen, making an unnecessary clatter with the pans. Worry always made him noisy. Storm's empty plate stood on the kitchen table, and Paddy Joe remembered how he had left it dirty only a few days before, having more important things to do, from his own viewpoint. If only he had done as he was told.

He washed his hands at the deep sink. He had

thought it odd when he first saw it, deep enough to dip a sheep, with a shallow one beside it. Tomkin had said it was the only bath they had. Now he scarcely noticed it, and he dried his hands and went forlornly to his place.

No one looked at the hearthrug. No one spoke. There was nothing to say. Tomkin had prepared their favourite food, but it had no savour. Storm had been missing for more than nineteen hours, and hope was as tenuous as a rumour. The dog could not possibly be on the island or he would have heard them calling and have barked to draw their attention. Paddy Joe flung down his knife and fork. How could anyone expect him to eat? He went out into the garden and sat on the edge of the sundial and stared at the sea. He had no idea where to look.

10

That afternoon, the Colonel scoured the beaches, calling, while Paddy Joe and Tomkin hunted through the woods again. If Storm had been free he would have come back to them by now. He must be ravenous. So he must be trapped. He couldn't possibly be dead. Paddy Joe had visions of his dog caught between two rocks, or pinned under a fallen tree, or lying with a broken leg, trying to bark to them. They would not hear him. The wind had risen again and screamed in protest through the trees, tossing the branches. Frightened birds called although it was almost dark. The sea roared on the rocks. It was the wildest night that even Tomkin had ever known, and there was nothing to say as they turned and fought their way against the wind to the cottage, reaching it as rain lashed from a maelstrom of cloud, chased by a bellowing wind that made everything fly before it. The autumn gales were early, and one followed on the heels of another. Feeding storms, Andy called them. Paddy Joe would associate the island with wind all his life.

The sky darkened, jagged clouds, banked on the horizon, forming black curtains over the high hills. The mountains loomed, forbidding and bleak. A sulphurous light streaked the ranges, glowing eerily on sea and woods.

Far out beyond the Isles of the Sea, and the Holy Isles

71

beyond Staffa and Iona, the Atlantic lifted itself into high swells and seamen watched uneasily. Boats slipped back into Tobermory Bay, and into Oban harbour, running for shelter. The sky came down until it met the sea, cloud piled high on black angry cloud. A false sunset coloured the peaks and the waves crashed on the beaches.

The first sign of change came, along with the lightning that flashed blue on the far horizon, sheeting the sky with frequent light. Thunder followed, echoing and re-echoing from hill and hollow and rocky mountain peak. Paddy Joe thought miserably of his dog. Storm hated lightning, and tried to shield his eyes, hiding them behind his paws. He did not mind noise. He was used to guns, and thunder did not frighten him, but the bewildering light was so brilliant that it hurt. Paddy Joe hoped his dog was hidden in the dark, away from the blue flashes that blazed out of the stricken sky.

He listened to the wind. It had started gently, sighing mournfully, mounting within minutes to gale force, screaming across the sea, tearing over the island, dragging at the trees so that they bent and swayed in an agony of constant movement.

Even from the cottage window, he could see the creaming waves lashed to fury, thundering against resisting granite cliffs, creeping higher and higher, sucking away the débris of many tides, and spilling more.

Tomkin had forecast the gale because the gulls had gone from the beaches that afternoon, flying inland, aware of the falling pressure before it had time to register on the barometer. Their wheeling wings whirred over garden and park, and they alighted in field and pasture, out of reach of the terrible sea.

The beach beyond the cottage was stony, and the sea took the stones and flung them hard against the shore.

The night was hideous with noise, and Paddy Joe stood uneasily, listening to the wind racing through the trees, rejoicing loudly in its savage strength, hearing the sea hurtle itself on cliff and rock and sand and shingle, as if striving to suck the whole island into its greedy maw. Thunder rumbled again, reverberating over the hills; lightning flashed, revealing the dinghy. Tomkin saw it, and frowned.

'The tide's terribly high,' he said. 'And the wind's behind it. I think we'd better move the boat. And if the Colonel's not in soon, we'll need a search party for him.'

Paddy Joe followed Tomkin out into the night. It was impossible to speak. The wind took the words and tossed them away. He had thought that island life was fun, away from civilisation, dependent on yourself for everything. Now he was not so sure. The sound of the wind in the trees was terrifying, and he had never imagined that seas could be so tremendous. The waves flung themselves against the little cliffs and spray showered high in the air, so that soon they were met with salt water, and the intrusive wind, drying their skins, left a sting behind.

Lightning dazzled on the peaks, sheets of blue and red and amber; scything yellow forks zigged towards the earth, a continual bombardment of electricity. The noise reminded Tomkin of the war and he found himself ducking his head, expecting bullets to rain around him. Paddy Joe could think of nothing but his dog, alone in the wicked darkness.

A new torment waited as they tried to lift the boat. The wind mocked them, bellying the tarpaulin that covered it; it tried to tug the boat from them, and twice Paddy Joe fell, his feet sliding in the mud. The second time he caught his hand painfully between the stern of the dinghy and the sharp edge of a rock, and cried out in pain, but nobody heard the sound, not even he. Somehow they managed to lift the boat, and drag it over the wall and carry it to the garden, stopping frequently to get their breath, and rest. The tarpaulin, unfastened at one end, was snatched away from them, and taken to sea, flapping with horrid noise until it fell on the water, and was soaked and vanished. Tomkin went back for the outboard motor, while Paddy Joe took cover in the porch, and waited. He did not want to go into the empty cottage. There was no dog to greet him, wagging a frantic tail in welcome.

The rain was falling in long straight ribbons that soaked both of them within minutes. Paddy Joe had forgotten that his tent was in the back garden. It must have been blown down too, as the polythene which he used as a ground sheet came twisting towards him. He ran round to the back of the cottage and found the tent lying in a tangled heap, the wind prisoned inside it, struggling like a live thing to get out.

There was nothing to be done. He weighted the canvas with heavy rocks taken from the beach, carrying each one grimly, battling against the wind. Tomkin helped him, and they rescued the sheeting which was plastered against the cottage wall. It was surprising, Paddy Joe thought suddenly, how much you could see once your eyes were accustomed to the dark. It was not really completely dark, at all. The din of the sea, the roar of tumbling rocks, the howl of the wind and persistent thunder rumbles were a bewildering background, deafening both of them. Paddy Joe thought of his dog, and his misery deepened.

There was a bright glow in the sky, spinning towards them.

'Fireball,' Tomkin said. 'Duck.'

He dragged Paddy Joe down beside him, flat on the ground, and the glare vanished. A bombardment of sound followed as a pine tree was stripped of bark and split by lightning, so that it was left, two bare fingers pointing starkly to the sky, mute testimony to the terror of the night. Paddy Joe shook his head and tried to clear his ears. He had never heard such a crash. Tomkin reached out a reassuring hand and gripped the boy's shoulder. Speech was impossible.

They went indoors. Tomkin banked the fire. Paddy Joe stripped off wet clothes and towelled himself dry, and came down again to find Tomkin was heating soup, muttering to himself, disturbed because the Colonel was still searching the island in the dark.

'No fool like an old fool,' Tomkin said, deft hands setting the table. 'He'll catch his death. I only hope . . .'

But he did not say what he hoped. Paddy Joe went to the window again and looked out at the night, and wished the gale would die away and let him hunt for his dog again. He did not want to eat. He felt too unhappy.

The Colonel came in half an hour later, his face grim, his eyes tired. He looked at Paddy Joe. There was no need for words. No dog followed him. He took off his soaked coat and stretched cold feet to the blaze that Tomkin had made in the hearth. Paddy Joe crouched on a stool, his face white.

'Bed, Paddy Joe,' the Colonel said. Paddy Joe looked up at his guardian, brown eyes pleading. He knew he would not sleep.

'There's nothing more we can do tonight,' Tomkin saw the glance and interpreted it correctly. 'We'll hunt for Storm again in the morning, and get Mac and Andy on the job too. They know every inch of the island. Likely he went down a foxhole and got stuck. We'll find him.'

Paddy Joe went to his room. He undressed slowly, dropping his clothes on the floor, walking to the window time and again to look into the darkness, and watch the rain sheeting down the window pane. Rumbling thunder grumbled in the distance. There was no pleasure in anything without his dog. If Storm were there they would have romped together, and he would have talked to the Alsatian, aware of listening ears that seemed sympathetic, even though Paddy Joe knew perfectly well that his dog did not understand the words, but only the familiar tones from which he took comfort. Storm loved attention and hated to be ignored, and conversation was attention. He had been missing for two nights and a day. Hope was fading.

Paddy Joe dragged on his pyjamas and climbed into bed. The bed was high, and the floor so old that it gave beneath his feet, so that more than once he had wondered if he would go through. Rot everywhere, the Colonel had said. Dry rot and wet rot too and the walls were damp and the roof leaked in the corner. Tomkin had put a bucket to catch the drips and Paddy Joe heard the maddening clang clang of each drop and remembered the old Japanese torture, of water falling, drip by slow drip, on a man's head.

The wind was frightening. There was a rip and tear, and an unpleasant slither as a slate slid from the roof, and fell with a sharp crack and a clatter of broken pieces. Paddy Joe wondered if the roof would come right off, and, as he listened to the wind fling itself among the groaning branches, and heard the leafy roar, he wondered if a tree would crash down on the cottage, or if it would crash down on Storm, or if Storm already lay dead under a fallen trunk. Sleep was impossible. He climbed out of bed again and found his torch, and his copy of *Lord of the Rings*, and turned to it for comfort. It had been his grandmother's favourite book and she often said that it was a reflection of life in many ways. Something was sure to turn up in time; someone else had said that too. Was it Dickens? He could not remember, but trying to remember was better than listening to the wind, or thinking about Storm.

Tomkin, looking in later, found Paddy Joe asleep, his book under his hand, the torchlight burning low as the battery was dying. The man turned it off and moved it to the bedside table, sighing. He himself was not sure that they would find the dog in the morning. Something must have happened to prevent the Alsatian joining them. Tomkin thought of the encroaching sea, of the howling wind, of the branches tossed contemptuously through the air, and sighed again as he shut the door. Poor little nipper; growing up wasn't much fun. Nothing lasted for ever. Pity that dumb beasts didn't have a longer life. Tomkin had lived through so many cats and dogs and even horses, and he never did get used to losing them. Time healed, and another pet came to take the lost animal's place, and the newcomer had his own endearing ways and you were soon fond of it, though you vowed never again. But there was always a small place left that didn't quite heal, a little space filled with sorrow.

Tomkin had many such places in his mind; memories of a ginger cat he had as a boy; of his first dog, a lurcher named Pat; of the horse he rode during the war; and a tiny corner for a hedgehog that he had kept for almost six months also during the war. He had been in a miserable billet, sleeping in a dilapidated hut, and the hedgehog had come daily for bread and milk, and taken bits of vegetable from Tomkin's hand. He'd called it Fred, and it had suddenly upset all his calculations by disappearing for three weeks and arriving with a tow of tiny hedgehogs, absurd little bright-eyed things that had not trusted him at all. He had re-named the mother Freda, and been sorry to leave her behind when he moved on. She had brightened many dreary hours with her absurdities.

Tomkin glanced out of his own bedroom window. Where was the dog? He did not know, and he was far from happy as he in his turn climbed into his brass studded bed, and lay listening to the sounds that raged outside the window. No wonder legends spoke of the wild hunt. It was easy to imagine a demon huntsman and a demon band racing through the trees, screaming as they chased some poor storm-bound creature. It was long before Tomkin slept.

In his own room the Colonel sat in the creaking basket chair, sucking on an empty pipe. He was giving up smoking, but it was not easy. Tomkin had persuaded him. Tomkin did not smoke, saying it was a disgusting habit, and when the reek from the pipe floated on the air, he wrinkled his nose, coughing in protest.

The Colonel, too, knew the emptiness left when a dog or cat had died. He laid the pipe on the table and walked to the window. The view did not reassure him, and he undressed as slowly as Paddy Joe had done, and lay watching the leaves sway and swoop and sweep the panes of glass between the leading, as the wind tried to tear them from the trees. It was a night to believe in ghosts and devils, a night to be thankful for indoors and a roof over a man's head. A night to pray for ships tossed on the waves, and men working on their decks to keep them afloat on seas that terrified anyone that saw them. It was not a fit night for a dog to be out. And there was no comfort in that old saw, either.

Some hours later, Paddy Joe woke and reached out his hand, and found nothing. He jumped up, remembering. The wind had eased, though the sea still fought the land and roared on the rocky beach. 'Storm,' Paddy Joe whispered. 'Storm.' His eyes hurt and felt hot and tight and his throat ached. He walked to the window. Dawn was a hint of grey light on the far horizon. The clouds bulked dark, and rain dripped drearily from the leaves. There would be no more sleep that night. Paddy Joe dressed, and went downstairs, and eased the big bolt on the heavy door, and opened the door a crack and slipped outside, closing it softly behind him. He was going to look for his dog again. He shivered in the chilliness of daybreak, and set his teeth, and went out into the turmoil, fighting for his breath. Storm. Storm. Storm. Where are you, he whispered inside his head and willed himself desperately to pick up a tremor, a thought from the dog, a hint of his direction. Storm could not be dead.

11

That day Paddy Joe knew despair and no one could comfort him. Both the Colonel and Tomkin were convinced the dog was dead. Storm had vanished as completely as if he had never existed. The weather had changed again. It was hot on the beach. The island brooded in a breathless stillness that presaged more thunder, the sea was glassy smooth and mirror clear. Paddy Joe looked across to the mountains crouched on the mainland, their peaks hard and black against the skyline. The mountains dived into the sea. There was a flat rock out in the loch and on it a dark shape. It might be Storm. He might have swum out, looking for Paddy Joe, and been too exhausted to swim back. Tomkin had left the boat so that it floated, its painter tied to a large post at the edge of the jetty.

Paddy Joe untied the painter and unshipped the oars. He rowed for a few yards. It was deep here, with a steep shelf dipping down sharply just beyond the sandy bottom, and so clear that Paddy Joe could see to the edge of the steps, and see the water darken and shadowy fish slide along the overhang and vanish. He wished he could skin-dive, and tried to imagine the seal's world, among waving weed and moving fish, and giant jellyfish. Beyond him, on the rock, the dark shape was moving. It was the right size for a dog. Paddy Joe was sure it was his dog. He began to row faster, pulling hard on the oars, thrusting the boat through the water. There were road builders working on the other side of the loch, making a new motorway that would lead tourists direct to the ferry to the Isles. The road bent away from the water, and, as he watched, a cloud of dust eddied into the air, followed by a dull explosion.

There was a seethe of movement, a slide and slip and flurry and splash and slap, and the shape slid hastily into the loch. Paddy Joe watched and saw a seal pup's head, as he swam through the waves, his wake creaming behind him. He somersaulted twice, and then made for the open sea. Paddy Joe had never known such disappointment. A cormorant dived suddenly, and rose with a fish in its beak, and flapped off heavily. A heron fished on the beach, its long legs splayed, its body motionless. The grey feathers were slightly ruffled. Eyes watched and the long beak waited. It was as still as the unbroken sky-reflecting sea that lay oily and sullen, the threat of wild weather implicit in its depths.

The sky was split with sudden light. Zigzags etched the dark clouds that gathered over the peaks, and thunder threatened and boomed. Within seconds the sky was black and the sea stirred angrily, a long swell rolling unexpectedly through the neck of the loch, building so swiftly that, before Paddy Joe had time to realise what had happened, the boat was rocking, angry waves were piling round him, and he was unprepared. Tomkin had warned him, and he had forgotten everything he had been told. Just as he'd forgotten to train his dog and as a result they were both in danger. If only Storm were alive. But that was a thought he dared not face.

He had broken every rule in the book. He had gone out alone. He had not told anyone he was going. He had not watched the weather, or he would have seen the thunderheads building in the mountains. He should have seen the squall bear down from the end of the loch; he should have noticed the distant white caps on the waves; he should have seen the slow swell rolling in from outside. He could have kicked himself.

There was no time for that. He looked at the shore. Tide and wind were against him and he was drifting out into the wildest part of the loch. He was not so far from the shore, but the tide had turned and the current was fierce, and set towards the mainland. There was no chance of swimming. He dropped the anchor, kneeling in the bottom of the boat, weighing it out with immense care.

He was safe enough so long as he stayed still. So long as the crashing waves did not overturn them. The beach seemed unbelievably far away. He could not row ashore. He dared not move the boat. He dared not move himself. He could do nothing.

Paddy Joe crouched on the bottom-boards. He was furious with himself. What a fool! What an utter, stupid, purblind idiot. He was safe enough if he stayed there, huddled in the bottom of the boat, rocking and tossing only a hand's reach from safety, but he was cold, and with the wind had come heavy rain that drummed on the surface of the sea, and soaked him. And he felt sick. And Tomkin would be furious with him, and the colonel would be sad, and that was just as difficult to bear.

He had never realised how rough the sea could get. Tomkin always made certain that they were ashore if bad weather threatened. The sea-rip tore a white line of foam beyond the end of the jetty. Thunder pealed across the peaks. Rain soaked from an overall mass of thick grey cloud, dark as the unshorn fleece of an old ewe, and as ragged and shaggy. The wind ripped the clouds apart, and rammed them together again, and lightning scythed across the peaks and flashed on the mountains, and a continuous grumbling rumble sounded terrifyingly close.

If only he had never gone out in the boat. If only Tomkin would come, but there was nothing Tomkin could do. There was not another boat near. Suppose the waves overturned the dinghy? Rain, lancing from the sky, laced with stinging hailstones, was collecting in the bottom of the boat. Suppose it filled and sank. Suppose no one knew he was here. Would anyone ever guess? Would Tomkin or the Colonel look for him? Or would they hunt as they had hunted for the dog, and have to wait until the sea tossed his body on the shore and flung the remains of the boat on to the rocks? Sick or not, he had to bale.

Paddy Joe shivered, and not only with cold. He was desperately afraid. He was much more alone than if he had been lost on land. There was always a house, or he could go to a police station. Now he was imprisoned, unable to shout and attract attention, and afraid even to look at the shore where breakers pounded ruthlessly against the low cliff edge, and spray leaped high and cascaded into the water again, and the noise was the noise of a million demons, fighting a battle to end all battles. Fighting the last battle of the evil creatures of the dark mountain. If he thought hard enough about that perhaps he could forget the sea.

But the sea would not let him forget. Soon he was very sea-sick, and lay, crouched in misery, on the wet floor. If only the movement would stop. If only the sea would subside. If only the waves were smaller.

He had thought things could not get worse, but they could. The sky was midnight black although it was not yet dusk. Darkness hid mountains that shouldered out of low cloud, and vanished again, and were hidden for good. The rain was torrential, and it was bitterly cold, and only a brief while before it had been so hot that

Paddy Joe had shed his shirt to sunbathe. That was now sodden, a useless bundle of rag that had neither shape nor warmth. Paddy Joe was sure he would die of exposure before the storm ended.

The boat was a flimsy shell flung from wave top to wave top. It was small protection against the sea, and no protection against the weather. Never, ever again, would he go in a boat, Paddy Joe vowed. If only he got safely ashore and found his dog he would always do as he was told. He would always think hard before he acted. He would never do anything so foolhardy again. He did not see Tomkin come to the water's edge and look, and go away again. He was too sick to lift his head, too cold to care, and the shivers that racked him were uncontrollable.

There was a noise above the screaming of the wind. The trees in the wood were creaking and straining, their boughs lifting high in the air and then flinging themselves sideways and downwards, and above the howling wind and the tear and crack of the trees came the cries of terrified birds. Chatter of jay and magpie, scream of heron, alarm call of starling. Rook and crow, raven and pheasant, pigeon and dove, hawk and kestrel, crying out against the din and the crash and the soaking chill of rain that flailed soft skin and sleek feather and left them draggled lumps of misery, under leaves that poured more water on them than came from the skies above.

Small creatures hid in holes. The fox crouched underground, the wildcat fled for sanctuary, and Paddy Joe hated Scotland, and hated its wild weather and hated the late summer and the frequent gales.

He dozed, and dreamed he was being shaken over and over again by a giant hand and cried out, and woke to see a searchlight flashing across the water. He sat up, staring. It was dark, and the roar of wind and waves was unabated, but the light swerved and turned towards him and held the boat in its glare, and approached steadily.

The voice coming from the night was total comfort. 'Lifeboat here,' it boomed above the sea. 'Stand by to catch a rope.'

Paddy Joe was so cold that the rope slid into the sea the first time, but the second time he held it and fastened it. Soon capable hands were grabbing him, and he was lifted aboard the lifeboat, the sea and tipping boat making the transhipment almost impossible, a muddled welter of waves and wind, so that Paddy Joe was never sure how he had actually reached safety.

He was taken into the little cabin, rubbed with a rough towel, wrapped in warm blankets and given a small cup of water and glucose to drink.

'Have to warm up slowly, lad,' a big man said, looming above him. 'If we give you anything hot we can shock you. Take it easy now.'

Paddy Joe took it easy. He finished his drink, and was thankful to lie on the bunk, and think of nothing at all. He did not know when he was taken ashore. He did not feel the movement of the car, or see the Colonel's anxious face. He did not know that Tomkin had lifted him out of the car and carried him upstairs and put him to bed, nor did he wake when the doctor called. The hours in the boat had exhausted him completely and he was cold and shocked and slept like the dead.

12

Paddy Joe slept, unaware of time passing. He did not know that Mac and Andy and the man from the garage were searching the island. He did not know that the Colonel had worn himself out, hunting and calling. He did not know that there was an advertisement in the local paper, asking if anyone had seen a straying Alsatian.

Tomkin looked into the room several times, his face grim. Paddy Joe was a responsibility. He was too impetuous; he rarely stopped to think. He should never have taken the boat, even if he did believe the dog was marooned on the rock. He should have come back to the house to tell Tomkin. He would have been discouraged, even then, as the storm that was building was plain for anyone to see who had eyes.

'Ye canna expect auld heads on young shoulders,' Andy said, when Tomkin voiced his worry. 'The lad's safe and now we hae to find his dog. It would be a pity to lose it.'

Tomkin made beef broth, and skimmed off the fat, and set the liquid aside for Paddy Joe when he should wake. The boy would be suffering for his foolishness and the worse for his ordeal. He was lucky to be alive. Out in the loch in that weather. Tomkin shivered. He did not want to remember his feelings when he had gone down to look for Paddy Joe and seen the little dinghy tossing high on the waves and the small head in the bows. Boys!

The long day wore past. The Colonel came home exhausted, and sat by the fire, gazing into the flames, knowing that he would have to tell Paddy Joe there was no longer any hope. The dog had either left the island and was running wild, or was dead. There was no other possibility. He had been lost for over four days.

Mac and Andy came into the kitchen, the merriment missing from their faces.

'I mind once a terrier that was trapped in a fox-hole, and rescued well and alive six days later,' Mac said. 'Maybe the dog went after the fox.'

'More likely he's gone wild and gone to the mainland and is killing sheep,' Tomkin said sourly. 'The old lady bought him for the boy. He was a stray. No one knows anything about his ancestry and Alsatians can go bad.'

'So can collies,' Mac said. 'There's a killer dog on the mainland now, and he's farmer's dog. Run off and gone wild. Bad blood in him. Everyone is out with guns.'

That was a new hazard. If Storm were running free . . . Tomkin did not want to face Paddy Joe. The boy doted on the dog. Tomkin felt sour. He was furious with Paddy Joe, and he was even more furious with himself. He had been unfair and he should have reminded the boy to keep up the dog's lessons. As Mac had said, there was little use in expecting an old head on young shoulders. It was his fault too that the dog had strayed.

The Colonel was thinking on much the same lines. It was a big responsibility, taking on the boy, and he felt too old. Paddy Joe was young, was impulsive, and it was hard to remember how boyhood felt. A stray memory caught at the Colonel's mind, and he suddenly saw himself, ten years old, anxious to go fishing, while his father dallied and gossiped to neighbours, and at last, impatient to be away, he had run off alone and tumbled into the river. There had been a great to-do about that. The years fell away and the Colonel was ten again, listening to his father railing in fury about foolhardiness. Poor Paddy Joe. The Colonel picked up his pipe and tamped it full of tobacco. He caught Tomkin's acid glance, and sucked the unlit pipe, deriving little comfort. The hearthrug looked bare, without the dog.

Paddy Joe slept through breakfast and he slept through lunch. He woke uneasily when darkness was more than a hint outside the window. Tomkin had lit the oil lamp and was standing by the bed, a tray in his hands. He wanted to rail at Paddy Joe, but the lad had had a sharp lesson. Tomkin said nothing.

'Have you found Storm?' Paddy Joe asked.

Tomkin shook his head. Paddy Joe took the steaming mug and began to sip. He ached all over. He was hungry, and he was reluctant to face the shadows beyond the lamp. The darkness brought fear. Fear of being alone without his dog for the rest of his life. Fear of shadows. Fear of growing up. Nothing was predictable.

'No dog lives for ever, Paddy Joe,' Tomkin said.

Paddy Joe knew that, but his dog was only three years old. If he were dead it was all Paddy Joe's fault. When Tomkin had gone downstairs again Paddy Joe faced the shadows, but they offered no comfort. The world was cold and bleak and unfriendly and he belonged nowhere. The Colonel and Tomkin had been better off without him. He should have gone to the boys' home. And his dog should have been put to sleep. Then at least he would know what had happened to him.

The room was dim and misty and the shadows flickered and danced, and Paddy Joe dozed again. The ache inside him was worse. The loneliness was inescapable. He needed his dog. He could not sleep. He could not rest. He could not wait, wondering. He must get up. He must do something, anything. Life was unbearable without Storm.

Paddy Joe climbed out of bed. His legs were wobbly and his knees felt weak. He pulled on his clothes.

Tomkin and the Colonel were eating their evening meal in the kitchen, and they did not see Paddy Joe pass swiftly through the shadows of the hall. The front door swung open, and shut with scarcely a sound, and a swift chill blew through the house and the two men shivered.

'Someone walking over my grave,' Tomkin said, with a half laugh. He was not often superstitious, but somehow, tonight, the island felt uncanny and had an atmosphere about it that he did not trust. Odd things happened on the island. Mac and Andy had said so, but they did not say what.

'I wonder where the dog went,' the Colonel said. They could think and talk of little else.

'Another dog vanished from the island,' Tomkin said. 'Paddy Joe said his name was Glenn.'

'And how did Paddy Joe know that?' the Colonel asked.

Tomkin did not answer. How had the boy known? He went to shut the kitchen door and then, on an impulse, went up the stairs to look at the boy, and found only an empty bed and Paddy Joe gone and his pyjamas lying on the floor.

'The boy's gone too,' Tomkin said, and the Colonel set aside his plate and fetched a torch and the two went out into the dark. There was no moon and the wind teased mournfully among the branches and a thin rain was falling. Anger mounted again. Paddy Joe was impossible. An utter young idiot. He didn't even learn.

'The boy's daft,' Tomkin said irritably, but the Colonel did not answer. The boy wanted his dog. He was lonely for its company. Pity walked beside the Colonel as he searched the empty woods.

Paddy Joe went out of the house like a sleep walker. He followed a beaten track between the trees. The woods were wet and dismal; rain dripping from the autumn-weary leaves, rain falling with soft plaint on the ground, rain damping Paddy Joe's hair and clothes. He was unaware of the weather. He moved carefully, avoiding the heavy trunks, and ignored the water that was seeping into his shoes.

He was a shadow moving among other shadows, walking down the gentle slope that led to the beach on the far side of the island. A calling owl startled the dark. Its soft wings brushed the night. Its silent shape winged towards the farm. Its mate answered, her cries ghostly. Owl call answered owl call and Paddy Joe walked on.

'Storm!' He whispered. Nothing moved. A moment later his foot slipped, and he knew he was in trouble again. There was no room for fear. The ground was treacherous, with pitfall and bog, and Paddy Joe was knee deep in mud, floundering to get out. Desperate, he nerved himself, remembering Tomkin's advice. Think, Paddy Joe. Don't panic. He mustn't struggle or he would sink deeper. He caught at the edge of a sapling and pulled himself out of the mud. He shivered as the wind probed his clothes and struck against his skin with frosty promise. There was a faint sheen on the grass beneath his feet and the light was coming back to the island.

Paddy Joe came to the beach. He had never been to this side of the island. The Colonel had searched here, and Paddy Joe had not had time to explore. The shore was steeper than that near the cottage, grey granite cliffs dropping into a little cove. There was the sound of the wind all round him and the sound of the sea enclosed him and the high keen of seagulls hung on the air.

The place was desolate. No one had walked here, ever before. The sand stretched to the tide mark, clean and unbroken. Only the birds broke the solitude with their swift winged flight.

Paddy Joe looked all round him. Fear was an ache inside him. If only he could believe that he would find his dog. He sat, head in hands, staring at the beach. Now that he was here he might as well search, but he had no hope left. No hope at all. Above him the wheeling gulls screamed in mockery.

13

The sky lightened as day crept over the horizon. Shadows lay on the mountains, and the far-away peaks were shrouded in thick grey clouds that hid them from sight. The air was damp, but the rain had ceased. The wind still tormented the trees, and Paddy Joe, skirting the restless sea, saw the waves worry a thick tangled mass of seaweed and driftwood, dragging it down the beach only to fling it high again, and race away, returning in fury to snatch the weed back and fling it on the water.

The tide was falling, leaving behind it the debris of the gale. A line of sea wrack marked high water and caught among it were trees and branches and wreckage from a small boat, the name *Doreen* written on one plank; a half barrel, stripped clean and empty, lay on its side, and beyond was the dark back of some animal. A dead animal, lying beyond help and beyond time. Paddy Joe stared at it, and felt his throat thicken with horror. Storm.

Storm! He could not move. His unwilling feet dragged slowly towards the tree. Please, God, don't let it be Storm. Please. Please. Please. He could not look. He dared not bend over the battered body or see what the waves had done to his pet. He stood, staring at the sea, at the trees, at the line of weed, wishing it were yesterday, it were last week, it were last year, that Storm were running beside him, alive and full of excitement. He made himself look.

It was not Storm. A dead sheep lay against the tree, trapped by the water, flung to a pitiless death on the rocks. Paddy Joe shuddered. His legs were shaking with relief. He left the sheep and climbed the rock, bracing himself against the wind. His shoes slid on the wet surface. He took them off. Better not slip and break his ankle. He knew he should not have come out alone. It was too easy to fall, to crash down the steep-angled granite into the deep water beyond that lay waiting to engulf him, raging at the rock. He left the beach, knowing that it was safer in the wood. Or was it? Huge branches lay on the ground, ripped from the trees above. A giant elm leaned against the wind, its trunk creaking, its roots bared, the soil heaped against it.

The wind was dying. There were lulls now between the gusts, each lull a respite, each longer than the last. The clouds were breaking, soft blue and green showing between long dark streamers, and the wind had shredded the sky to rags that hung in tattered tendrils. Paddy Joe listened during the lulls, waiting for the familiar bark, or a soft whine, to show him where Storm was hidden.

He jumped as a bark sounded behind him, and spun sharply on his heel. Hope faded. A young roe hind stood with her first fawn at heel. She had seen Paddy Joe and barked to her baby. He moved slowly. He was not yet able to run as fast as his mother. Paddy Joe saw the dappled body shift in the shadows under the trees. He left the glade quickly, disappointment so violent that he had to blink away tears.

The wood ended on a spit of land that was surrounded on three sides by the sea. The wind had dropped, and the crash of waves on the beach dominated everything. Paddy Joe looked towards the rocks that spiked out of the sea. There was a cave at the end of the cliff, its entrance blocked by a long ago fall of earth and rock. Beyond the cave was hard ground, and the little hill that guarded the Nature Reserve.

Paddy Joe sat on a rock and watched the sea break in a flurry of spray that shot into the air. He was hungry. He had had very little supper the night before. He found a toffee in his pocket, soft and sticky with age, but it was better than nothing, and he ate it, and wished there were more. He stood up to return before he was missed, and then, in the act of moving, paused, eyes wide, head turning. He had heard a bark. It came from the little cove. He ran.

The ground was uneven and he tripped and fell, and resigned himself to moving more cautiously. It would not do to break a leg. He picked his way over the slippery, weed covered rocks. He shouted.

'Storm!'

This time there was no mistake. The dog's deep bay sounded from the rocks by the place that Mac and Andy called the Smugglers' Cave. It was muffled, as if it were underground, but it was vibrant, alive, excited. The dog was unharmed. Paddy Joe reached the rockfall and called again. This time the answer came from close by, and he found a fissure in the spillage, and tried to peer through. The dog barked in answer. He was inside, but how in the world had he got there? There wasn't a crack big enough for a squirrel, let alone an Alsatian dog.

Paddy Joe began to explore the fall. Once there had been a small slipway, up which a boat, and, possibly, a cargo could be dragged. When the tide was high there was deep water to the side of the slipway and iron rings bit into the stone. Paddy Joe came to the top of the slipway, and looked more closely at the rocks. One of them was wedged across a gap that looked as if it might allow him to bring the dog out if he could only move it. He looked carefully at the rocks around it, to make sure that he did not bring more rock on to his own head. They were all wedged securely. Paddy Joe pulled. The rock twisted under his hand and slid away so suddenly that he overbalanced and shot through the gap, and found himself falling. He landed with a jerk that sickened him, and rolled over as Storm came bounding towards him, barking eagerly, licking his hands and face over and over again, delighted to be re-united with his master. Paddy Joe looked up as pebbles rained down on him. The rocks had slipped again, and the entrance was blocked.

For a few minutes Paddy Joe gave himself up to pleasure. His dog was alive, was well, was not lying dead under a tree. Soon they would be out on the beach again, and he would race Storm back to the cottage and they would eat. He looked upwards.

He was in a small pit, the sides sheer, rising high above his head. He had fallen on sand. There was no chance at all of climbing out. And, he wondered, what chance was there of either Tomkin or the Colonel looking for him here? They might scour the island for hours and not find a clue to his presence. He was a fool. If he'd only thought. But it was too late now.

The only light shone through the crack by the hole he had just made by shifting the rock. It angled into the pit, leaving the base in darkness. There was an odd smell, a deep earthy underground smell, with an overhang of rankness that he identified as fox. How in the world could a fox get here? Yet Storm had come. There must be some other way in.

Paddy Joe began to explore. Three sides of the pit were smooth and sheer, but on the far side there was an opening big enough for him to stand upright. He could not see, but he stooped and felt the floor. Sand had drifted over it, but, when he brushed aside the sand, there was smooth rock. Someone had dug the passage, and it must lead somewhere. If only he had a torch.

He did not have a torch, but he did have Storm and Storm had a nose. He took the dog's collar, and said, 'Seek. Find Tomkin,' and Storm began to move into the darkness. He had wanted to get out into the light, and to find Paddy Joe, but now they were together and Storm trusted Paddy Joe, and obeyed him blindly. If Paddy Joe wanted to walk in the darkness, the dog was content to follow. Or to lead, as soon as it became plain that Paddy Joe had need of all Storm's senses. Once the boy banged his head on an overhang of the roof. Once he tripped over something that lay in his path. He needed his hands to guide him along the wall, and the farther he went the more sure he was that he was following a once well-known route. He wondered where it might end. It must have been used by smugglers. Perhaps at the end he would find treasure, though he was not at all sure what kind of treasure. The air was stale, and the smell of fox lay everywhere, so that it was no wonder that Storm had come hunting. The place must be riddled with foxes.

14

Paddy Joe had never known such darkness. There was not a glimmer of light. Nothing relieved the blackness. It was total, tangible, pushing against him, bringing a touch of terror with it. He had no idea what lay ahead. Perhaps there was a cave with a gaping hole in the floor, or, deep underground, some storeplace used by the long ago smugglers to hide illicit goods. Perhaps the sea entry was the only one, except for some narrow foxhole along which neither he nor Storm could creep. Storm was very big, even for an Alsatian. The dog pushed his nose against Paddy Joe's leg. It was reassurance.

There was darkness but not silence. There was creep and seethe and whisper and rustle. There was a rhythmic background murmur, at first unidentifiable, until Paddy Joe realised it was the sound of the sea on the beach. Suppose there was an entry to the tunnel along which the sea could rush and bury them deep in its icy clutch, and sweep out again, taking their bodies with it, or trap them here, where no one would ever know they'd come?

There was a sick taste in Paddy Joe's mouth. There was a thump in his chest that was caused by terror, a heart-racing terror that could not be stilled. He stopped walking and knelt on the floor and put his arms round his dog. Storm sat, patient, waiting. He had no idea why they were sitting there together in the dark. He had no knowledge of traps, and no fear, because he was with his master, and safety, for Storm, lay with Paddy Joe. He stretched and settled himself, nose on paws, to wait until unpredictable human whim should rouse him again.

Never give in to panic, Paddy Joe. Tomkin's voice might have been sounding beside him, he heard it so plainly. Paddy Joe sat down on the floor to try to think soberly, but it was not easy. He had no idea what lay in the dark. He had no knowledge of his direction, and only the sinister suck and swish of waves gave any clue to the nearness of the sea, and that was a mere inkling. Sometimes there was a sudden crash, as if the surf broke on solid rock, almost beside him. Sometimes there was only a dim seethe of water far away.

The wind was rising. It cried softly along the passage, whining like a beast in pain. Storm's ears were alert and his nose asked for news. It told him much and Paddy Joe wished the dog could speak. Storm was reading the air. He knew there was a fox prowling nearby. He had chased it once already, and followed it through underground tunnels until he reached the cave, where Paddy Joe found him. He had fed himself on its leavings. He knew the ground had a faint salty tang; he knew that no men had passed that way for longer than memory. He knew there was a musty smell, a smell he had never met before, a smell that set the ruff round his neck bristling, and drew his lips back in a silent snarl. He rested his head on Paddy Joe's leg and waited.

Take out your troubles and look them in the face and they'll vanish, Grandee had said. His grandmother was dead, but her words were imprinted on his memory. Nothing is as bad as you think it is. Thinking makes it worse. Do something about it. Paddy Joe felt an ache in his throat. Grandee had only been dead such a short while, and life had changed so completely since she was gone. But he had to grow up and face facts. After all, he was already twelve and would very soon be a man.

What did he fear? The sea. If the sea came through the passages regularly the sand underfoot would be damp. He put down his hand and felt dry dusty powder, that had lain there for days, for weeks, for years. The sea had never been in here. He felt the walls, and they were dry, coated with a soft powdery substance that tasted bitter on his fingers, so that Storm, licking the hand that lay near his nose, tried to lick away the taste from his tongue by licking his lips.

The sea was not an enemy, here. Paddy Joe sighed with relief. That was one worry less. But the worry about the exit from the passage was very real. There were several possibilities. The tunnel might end in a cellar under the old house. Or in a strong door, that was padlocked and bolted and could not be opened, where no one would ever look. It might end in a narrow fox-hole. It might come to a dead end through a fall of rock, or was there earth, buttressed with wood, like a mine entrance, above his head? Or was it a natural passage, leading from cave to cave?

There might be underground lakes. Or an inlet where the sea could surge. Did the floor slope up, or down? It was hard to tell. There was no sense of distance in the dark, or of level. He might have been sinking deep into a pit, or climbing towards the sky. He had no idea.

Whatever happened, he could not stay here, like a zombie, waiting for a miracle. It all depended on him, on him alone. Storm could use his nose, but he did not know what to ask Storm to find. No use telling the dog to seek Tomkin, as he would almost certainly return to the entrance through which Paddy Joe had crawled. No use saying home, as where was home? Not here, but several hundred miles away. Paddy Joe did not know if Storm would think of their cottage as home. Home meant the house where they had spent all their lives.

Paddy Joe jumped up, and at once the dog was eager attention. Together boy and Alsatian moved cautiously through the dark, the dog sniffing along an invisible trail, and Paddy Joe feeling with hands and feet, going gently, cautiously, aware that nothing here was safe or certain, that there might be a sudden rift that would catch a leg or trap both of them, or a drop in level that would break a bone, or just a blank wall, ending the trail.

Storm was aware of much more.

Darkness. Paddy Joe was always a little afraid of the dark, and the dark of a winter night was not so deep as this. Nothing broke the blackness. Outside at night you could see trees and the etched solidity of buildings, and the glim of the horizon and the orange glow above the towns, tell-tale from the street lamps. Indoors, the night glow sneaked through the curtains and the room was rarely so dark that nothing could be seen, and the beams of cars' headlamps shone on the ceiling. Light! Paddy Joe craved it more than he had ever craved food or drink. To see again, to see the shapes of trees, and clouds over the skies, and the green translucent depths of moving water.

To delight in colour; in the kingfisher sheen of feathers, the sharp yellow of egg-yolk, the green of lettuce, and the bright glow of gold-red tomatoes, and the purple lustre on a grape. That thought was a mistake. Hunger suddenly lurched and gripped. It had been hours since Paddy Joe ate.

He tore his thoughts away from food. He scanned the walls, but there was not a glimmer, not a flicker, not a trace of silver. Fish were silver. Fish were food and Paddy Joe's mouth was suddenly aswim with saliva and he knew how Storm felt when he was hungry and food too long in preparation, or too hot to put down for the dog. Down here, in the dark, nothing counted but blind instinct. Blind. This was how it felt to be blind. Never to see the sky or the colours of trees, never to know how people looked when they smiled, or the gentleness in friendly faces or the warm glow in a dog's eyes. Never to see how fur on a kitten blended softly and lay sleek or how food looked on a plate.

Steak and kidney, richly brown, with golden sweetcorn and fried potatoes. Yellow, turning to brown, with Tomkin adding more. Paddy Joe licked his lips. Every thought in his head led to food.

He forced himself to concentrate. The ground remained level and firm and sandy. He must be deep underground. He was totally lost, and he must find some way to get out. He reached towards the roof. It was there, just above him, solid, unbroken, and rock. A thin wind needled his hair. It was the first stir of air that he had felt, the first gleam of hope, the first sign that there was a break, somewhere. Ahead of him footsteps rustled the dry sand covering the uneven floor. Storm growled.

Footsteps! Paddy Joe swallowed and stood stock-still. Were there ghosts in the unrelenting dark, the ghosts of men who had fought the French and who had smuggled for years, risking death in flimsy boats that few would take to sea today? Was there the ghost of Meg Campbell, wailing for her lost husband, or of the Black Hermit, haunting a place that might have been his? The footsteps were closer. Storm growled again.

Not a ghost. Surely ghosts were silent presences. But in books they clanked and moaned and groaned, and also he had read of a place where footsteps sounded heavily on the stairs, and no man appeared. Where was it? He had read it recently, and then, suddenly, he remembered. It was in Macclesfield where there were one hundred and eight steps near the Town Hall. No one had ever seen anything on the steps, but each night, when the sombre note of the church clock died away at midnight, faltering feet lagged heavily up the steps, pausing on each tread, and anyone passing felt an icy chill, but there was nothing to see.

It was not a thought that brought any comfort. Paddy Joe tried to drive it out of his mind by remembering an absurd rhyme that Tomkin had once taught him when he was very small.

As I was going up the stair,
I met a man who wasn't there,
He wasn't there again today,
I wish that man would go away.

The footsteps came on. They were fast steps, moving swiftly towards them. Storm growled again, a deep throat-rumbling angry noise, that made Paddy Joe wonder what on earth was coming towards them in the dark.

A moment later he knew. The fox had come into his den and smelled strangers. He was running to defend his home, his property, his lair, against intruders. He was small and lithe and swift and he was on his own territory, with right on his side. The need to fight dominated him.

Storm was the intruder, but Storm had Paddy Joe to guard, and Storm's need was as great as the fox's. The Alsatian snarled as the fox leaped. Paddy Joe moved his arm. He could do nothing, and he knew that snapping teeth could maul his hand badly. He could not see. He could not help. He was flattened against the wall and the twisting bodies brushed against him. He knew there was a tangle of dog and fox, he knew from the sounds that this fight might end in death, and he was as helpless as if he was tied hand and foot. He clenched one hand against the other, and wished that the fight would end, that he were safe above ground again, that Storm had never wandered. He did not, for one moment, regret that he had come to look for his dog. At least they were together.

The sounds in the dark were magnified out of all reason. It was not a fight between dog and fox, but between two giant beasts, their growling and barking echoing horribly. They were battling tigers, roaring lions, fighting dinosaurs. The air was vibrant with hate, with fury, with the fear of death. The two bodies rolled over the sandy floor, teeth sinking deep, until Storm suddenly found a tender place on the fox's neck, and bit with all his strength.

The fox pulled himself free. It had almost been a death bite, but not quite. Another minute and all would be over, and the animal knew he was vanquished. He loped away, and found a distant corner, safe in the dark, and lay licking his wounds, while Paddy Joe knelt beside Storm and felt for his dog anxiously. Storm was exhausted, lying flat on the ground, breathing heavily. Paddy Joe's hands moved carefully along the line of the Alsatian's head, along the prick ears, over his nose, along his flanks and back and hindquarters, and along his tail, and knew that the dog was covered in bites, some of them severe, needing immediate attention. His fingers were sticky with blood and his dog was exhausted. Paddy Joe crouched in the dark, and knew defeat.

15

Paddy Joe knelt beside his dog. Storm was too tired to move. His body ached and the bites hurt, and he had used a great deal of energy in the fight. Also it was nearly five days since he had been fed properly. He had eaten the fox's leavings. There were springs in the cave and water had kept the dog alive. Water and the will to survive.

There was a stir in the distance, a faint smell that grew stronger, a tremor in the air. Storm jumped up and Paddy Joe breathed deeply, thankful to find the dog's injuries were not as severe as he had thought. The quiver in the darkness came towards them, and there was a shrill squeaking, a high pitched, almost indecipherable noise, just audible to the boy, but very easily heard by the Alsatian, who lifted his nose and sniffed a musky scent unlike anything he had ever met before. He growled again.

Paddy Joe flattened himself against the wall as the sound and smell grew stronger. Something furry brushed against his face, and there was a flitter of wings. Bats! And where there were bats and foxes there must be an entrance. He wondered why the bats were moving now, by day, when they always came out at dusk, and did not guess that the fox had been so hungry he had gone hunting in the little cave where the small creatures hung from the roof in the darkness, and leaped towards them, trying to catch them.

They had flown from his rapacious jaws, and left him

baffled and hungrier than ever and stiff and sore from his wounds.

Paddy Joe drowned in bats. The smell of them was overpowering, choking him. The wave of air as they passed was foetid, a scent from the underworld, a scent that made Storm bark, his deep bay echoing, so that panic drove the flight along, and wings skittered, and small voices squeaked, and the place was vibrant with fear.

Paddy Joe could imagine nothing more horrible than standing there, in the dark, deep underground, while the mothlike bodies flew past his face. They were uncanny creatures. Paddy Joe thought they were like rats endowed with the power of flight, unsavoury vermin, beastly to contemplate. He had never met bats before.

There were millions of them. Flying here, flittering there, their leathery wings unbirdlike as they brushed against the rock. Paddy Joe fondled Storm's ears to gain assurance. He had entered a nightmare, and he wished it were a real nightmare for then he could wake up. Now, he had to go on. He had no choice. He was penned in an unsavoury prison that might lead nowhere in the end.

Memories began to plague him. Memories of books he had read, of stories he had seen on television, of newspaper stories about trapped cavers and pot-holers. He had often thought it would be fun to explore underground, but now he was not so sure. The explorers had a light, and knew where the entrance lay, and how to escape so long as nothing went wrong. He had not even a match.

And things could go wrong. Roofs might fall in. Water could flood from the sea or seep through the roof. There might be hidden pitfalls. There might be booby traps. Suppose there was a skeleton, and he fell over the bones? Suppose the ghosts of long ago men stalked in the darkness?

He shivered and felt for Storm's head and was reassured by the feel of soft fur and the hard skull beneath it, and by a quick upward movement and cold nose in the palm of his hand. Storm had been desperately miserable, alone in the dark. The dog needed human company and he needed Paddy Joe as much as the boy needed his Alsatian. Paddy Joe was suddenly so overwhelmed with delight that he knelt on the floor and put his arms round his dog's neck and held him tight, and Storm licked the boy's face, revelling in company after the long hours of desolation. He had heard the Colonel calling and barked, but wind and sea had drowned the noise and the old man had not imagined that the dog could possibly be inside the fallen rock.

Slow step on slow step. Feel, and move, and feel again, using each foot cautiously, testing the floor, making sure that it was solid. Storm was moving warily too, his ears and nose testing for sound and scent, his whole body tense. He did not like the tunnel.

Paddy Joe was cold. He was not dressed for exploring underground. His thin jersey did little to keep out the chill. He wished he knew more about caves. He was still not sure whether he was inside a true cave system, or in a tunnel dug by human hands. There had been smugglers on the island, once. Ian Campbell had been a smuggler, so Mac and Andy said. It was better to think about that than to wonder how he was ever going to find a way out. Or how Storm had found a way in. But a way in must be there, and Paddy Joe was small and slender and could surely follow where the dog led? He was so busy thinking that he forgot to take care, and hit his head sharply on an overhang that dropped from the roof. He stopped, and sat down, feeling sick with pain. Storm licked his face.

The wall behind his back was rough. This was part of a true cave. Perhaps the smugglers had made their tunnels run into the natural ones. The floor beyond him sloped upwards sharply. For a moment he thought he could feel a sea breeze on his face and smell the tang, and the sound of waves was nearer. Then all was still again, and the darkness swept round him, so dense that he could feel it pressing on him, and he clung to the dog, needing reassurance.

Total darkness was terror. Darkness was fear, catching at the throat and thumping the pulses. Darkness hid unimaginable horrors. It hid the secrets of past ages. How old were the caves? Had monsters trodden the twisting passages? Had men fought and died here? Was that a footstep behind him in the silence? Paddy Joe held his breath and realised that the sound was blood racing as his pulse beat quickened. His mouth was full of saliva and he swallowed. He was very hungry and the ache in his middle intensified. He took hold of Storm's collar, and plodded on.

Step. And pause. And listen. Step, and feel, and stop. Breathing in the darkness. Storm's breathing and his own, but was there another breath behind it? An old verse came into Paddy Joe's head. Grandee had loved poetry and often read it to him. He half remembered the words, but had forgotten where they belonged . . .

As one who on some lonely road,
Doth walk in fear and dread,
As if he thought some awful fiend,
Did close behind him tread.

That was not quite right. Somewhere in the rhyme were the words 'Durst scarcely turn his head.' It was not a poem to remember in the dark.

Paddy Joe began to whistle. Whistling sometimes banished fear, but this time it did not. The sounds were eerie; an echo, lagging behind his own tune, came back to him as if someone else was catching the notes and flinging them away again.

A hymn might give him more courage. Paddy Joe knew a lot of hymns, from his school prayers each morning. He had forgotten all the songs he knew, and only the more mournful tunes came to mind. He sang softly as he walked.

'He who would valiant be 'gainst all disaster . . .'

That at least fitted in with his present situation. As he murmured the words he suddenly remembered the elusive quotation in full and that was no consolation either.

Like one that on some lonely road,
Doth walk in fear and dread,
And having once turned round walks on,
And turns no more his head,
Because he knows a frightful fiend,
Doth close behind him tread.

There was a soft thump in the darkness. Paddy Joe froze against the wall, every muscle quaking, and Storm growled. Nothing moved. Storm knew that a sea bird had come in through a tiny opening and landed on its nest. Paddy Joe never knew. He was to remember the incident for the rest of his life, standing there, immobile, not daring to breathe, lest something unearthly had come into the caves. The bird scratched a claw on rock, and Paddy Joe ran. He ran blindly, forgetting caution. He ran away from the unseen creature behind him. He ran until he was breathless, and Storm, pattering beside him, was puzzled by their headlong flight. It was only a bird. He could smell it, even now.

The floor was still rising, Paddy Joe slowed down, knowing he had been lucky not to tumble headlong over some obstruction in his path, or to run into an outcrop of rock projecting into the tunnel, or to blunder into water. He put his hand down and felt a narrow ledge. Storm, scenting water, began to lap. He was thirsty, and hunger was a pain so severe that it had vanished, gone beyond endurance. It was a long time since the dog had eaten.

There was a trickle of water running down the wall. Water was life, and Paddy Joe licked it. It tasted rusty and stale, but relieved the ache on his tongue and the need in his throat. Below him, Storm lapped until the rock was dry.

The tunnel was narrower and it was necessary to crawl. Paddy Joe felt fear snatch at his throat again. Suppose it ended in a blank wall and all his trouble had been for nothing. Suppose he could not get out? Suppose they could never get out? No one knew where he had gone. No one would know where to look for him. Years hence, someone else might blunder into the tunnel and find his bones. And those of his dog. They would wonder how they came there. Perhaps they would have heard stories about the island. About the sheepdog that vanished, and about the boy and his Alsatian who had come for a holiday and had disappeared as completely as if they had never existed. Queer things happened on the island. Mac and Andy said so.

The walls had drawn closer together. Crawling was a penance, but Paddy Joe had to go on. They could never find their way back to the other entrance now. There must be a way out. If only he had a light.

But there was no light. There was not a gleam to lighten the awful absolute dark. He had to trust to luck, had to feel his way over rock that was slimy to the touch, and Storm came behind him, his own legs half bent, his nose close against Paddy Joe's feet.

The tunnel twisted. Paddy Joe had to lie flat on his face and pull himself along and behind him Storm followed, determined to go where his master led. It was the most difficult thing that Paddy Joe had ever done. Suppose they were trapped here. Alone in the dark . . .

Please God. Let us get out of here. Please. Please. Ask and it shall be answered. Paddy Joe felt light-headed. This was worse than tossing in the boat. He could see then, even though water was all around him. It was worse than anything he had ever known. Worse than being ill. Worse than facing his headmaster when he had transgressed at school. Worse than Tomkin's cold anger. Worse than Grandee's death.

The narrow gap widened. Paddy Joe pulled himself through and his dog followed. There was cool air on his face. He looked up. High above him the moon's glim shone on a hole that led out of the ground. All around him the walls were sheer, and as he watched, earth trickled into one eye. He could never get out. And it was already night. He sat down, his back against the cold wall, and looked up at the shimmer. Storm dropped beside him, one paw on Paddy Joe's leg. Paddy Joe moved his hand. He shuddered and recoiled violently. He had touched bones. He could see the faint outline against the ground, and he moved away. There was a skeleton. The skeleton of some animal. Maybe a fox. Maybe a dog.

He was alone for ever, and there was no hope left at all. He could never climb those sides, or reach the opening. He and Storm would rot here, would starve in the darkness, and their bones would lie beside the bones that mouldered on the sodden ground.

Hope was a memory. Paddy Joe curled closed to his dog, thankful for the warmth of Storm's furcovered body, and desolation swept over him. There was nothing more he could do. He could not face the narrow tunnel again and once he was through it he did not know which way to go. Here at least there was a little light.

He was so tired that he slept, and his dreams were filled with terror. He ran through endless night, and footsteps sped behind him, accompanied by harsh breathing, but they never, quite, caught up.

16

By nightfall the Colonel was desperate and Tomkin was grim. Mac and Andy had scoured the island, had hunted the woods, had searched the little cliff path, had crossed the causeway and questioned the farmer and everyone else they met. It was no longer only a dog that was missing. It was also a boy.

'There's queer things happen on the island,' the man at the garage said, and that was poor consolation. As soon as he had finished for the day he shut the place up and joined the search. He brought the storekeeper and two fishermen with him, and the village policeman.

'We could do with a dog,' the policeman said, as they met in the cottage kitchen. Tomkin made hot coffee. No use everyone going without food. There were cold beef sandwiches. Paddy Joe would be hungry, too; if he were alive. Tomkin ate his own food but it tasted of nothing. Poor little fossil. The boy's life wasn't much fun. And the kid had missed his dog. If only he hadn't gone out alone. At least he wasn't in the boat this time. That was high and dry, safely above high water mark. But Paddy Joe was certainly a handful and his impulsiveness caused even more trouble.

'He might have fallen in the sea,' Mac said.

And if he had there was no hope of finding him alive, as it was high tide and a big sea running and the angry rip off the shore plain to even an unknowing eye. The wind was back and waves were breaking over the rocks in a flurry of foam. High tide had come and gone and come again, and there was no sign of the boy, anywhere.

The Colonel had retreated into silence and was wreathed in smoke. No use telling him not to smoke now. He wanted comfort and he wouldn't listen to Tomkin. He puffed away, as if his life depended on it. Smoke hung blue on the air and Mac coughed. He had a tender throat.

The men said nothing. There was nothing to say. All their thoughts followed the same lines. If he were alive, Paddy Joe was out there in the darkness, cold, hungry, and almost certainly alone. They had given up all hope of finding the dog.

The policeman was racking his brains, trying to remember the hazards on the island. There were too many. The deserted mansion attracted the mainland boys, and two had fallen from the gaping walls, having tried to climb them, and take illegal birds' eggs. They had paid dearly for their sins. One had broken his leg, and the other had cracked his skull. Both had been in hospital for weeks. Lads, the policeman thought sourly. They were always in trouble. Stuck up trees, or falling off roofs, or being caught by the tide, or marooned on a sandbank when the water came roaring in. They caught their heads fast in railings; they fell in bogs; they got lost. They never thought of the lost time and trouble they caused; or the financial cost of finding them.

Mac was wandering in the past, trying to remember the tales he had heard about the island. It had an unlucky history, between the Black Hermit and Ian Campbell and his unhappy wife, left widowed and alone, and growing old and strange. The lass from the store said she had seen Mistress Campbell sitting painting on the sea wall, with gulls whirling round her head, but Mistress Campbell had been dead for this

113

many a year, before the girl was born. Yet the lass had been positive.

The Colonel had called until he was hoarse, called until the echoes rang, called until he was sure that the words would lie on the air for ever.

'Paddy Joe. Where are you? Can you hear me? Paddy Joe?'

Nothing answered but a single bird, a desolate keen that sighed on the wind and marred the air, and terrified the senses. Nothing moved. No sign of the boy on hilltop or on beach. The Colonel had walked along the shore, staring at the ever-narrowing stretch of sand, looking for footsteps. Only sea-birds had walked in the sand.

It was impossible to search in the dark. The policeman left, to telephone to his headquarters and ask for a dog handler and a dog. They had a four-hour journey to make to the island. There was no dog near.

Andy stared miserably at the fire. He was a superstitious man, and believed wholeheartedly that ill luck came to anyone living on the island. The Island Luck, he called it. When he heard that a man had been hurt he would say,

'Ah weel, he has Island Luck.'

Island Luck was ill luck. Was haunting and disappearance. Was uncanny and was chancy. Mac and Andy lived on the mainland and nothing would persuade them, ever, to set up their home on the island. Shades of the Black Hermit and of his daughter roamed and cried in the night.

An owl called and called again. Bird of evil, bird of ill-will, bird of darkness. Andy crossed his fingers. He needed to ward off bad luck. The Colonel dozed, his head nodding uneasily in the big chair, and he woke again and shifted the cushion and closed his eyes. Worry had aged him, and Mac looked at him with concern. He was too old to have a lad to care for. But maybe he no longer had the lad at all. Mac was suddenly angry. He kicked at the log in the fireplace and it flared in a flurry of sparks. The side fell away, leaving dead ash, that glowed red and died to grey.

Voices whispered in the dark and shadows moved. The voices were those of creaking wood; the shadows were flung by the dying flames, but for all that Andy became increasingly uneasy. He believed in ghosts and demons and in the Little Men of the Hills, who, he was sure, were responsible for many odd things that happened. He could see them vividly when he tried; he was a man who saw visions. He would never walk on the battlegrounds, where men had fought and men had died and he swore that the air was anguished with the terror of long ago heroes. The wee bit moor beyond the island was an ill enough place. Stragglers from Culloden had fought there, and horses and ponies shied and bolted at the gate and the fox gave it a wide avoidance, and dogs hated the place. Andy hated it too.

Tonight he hated the cottage. He had never been there at night before and he made an excuse and went out into the garden where the wind sobbed in the trees and the waves moaned on the beaches, and the owl called to its mate. Outside the oppression lifted and the dark was friendly and familiar, an outdoor dark, not an indoor dark where unknown creatures hid behind the solid furniture and the memories of long ago folk sorrowed the spirit. Andy shivered, but not from cold.

Mac thought of the island. Thought of the old tales of smugglers; of the Black Hermit and of his daughter; thought of the story of buried treasure that was told in the villages on the mainland. Ian Campbell was supposed to have hidden a fortune somewhere before he died. Perhaps there was a secret room in the old house. Perhaps Paddy Joe had found it. Mac went back to the mansion and spent the lonely hours of the night tapping the falling walls. He disturbed nothing but two rats and a hundred assorted spiders. By dawn he was bone weary, as he tramped back along the weedy drive towards the cottage.

Andy had vanished, gone to chase an idea of his own. The Colonel was asleep, sitting in the arm-chair by the fire that Tomkin had just coaxed to a blaze. Tomkin was grey faced, and his eyes were shadowed and he needed a shave. He rubbed his hand across a blue-stubbled chin and looked across at Mac, his mouth voicing a soft question.

Mac shook his head.

Tomkin turned back to the fire and held out his hands to warm the chill that had suddenly overcome him. The Colonel woke and stared about him, startled to find himself dressed, sitting in the kitchen, and Tomkin could not bear the expression on the old man's face. He went outside to fetch more wood, and washed and shaved, and by the time he had boiled the kettle and cooked eggs and bacon and brewed a pot of tea, he was his own man again.

He looked outside the window, at the sea. It was a grey day, mist creeping over the horizon, blotting out the mainland. It was a dreary day, a day for misery, a day for despair.

A dog barked outside.

Everyone turned to look at the doorway. Footsteps sounded on the path, and Tomkin's hopes, which had been raised by sudden expectation, died again. The policeman stood in the doorway with the handler and his dog beside him. It was the wrong dog.

17

A cold day, a grey day with a thin mist falling. A seep of mist on the sodden grass, and the trail stone cold. The policeman had little hope. Like enough the lad was in some pit, or maybe run off to the mainland, looking for his dog. For all that he was a conscientious man, and he let his Alsatian cast about to find a trail.

Scent lay faint on the ground. Tam was a good dog, renowned for his nose and his ability to pick up the least trace of a track, long after other dogs had failed. He was a hard dog and too sharp by far to trust in a crowd, but he had no equal in tracking. He set off now at a good fast pace, across the island and on to the beach, where he nosed and nosed again at the cliff fall, and barked.

Paddy Joe had shifted the rocks to slip through, and then they had shifted again. There was no sign of any space through which a boy could pass.

'The dog's mistaken,' Tomkin said, grim faced. The policeman nodded. The boy might have been there, might have climbed the fall, but there was no way in. That was for sure. He pulled the dog off, but the dog was positive.

'Ye daft beast,' the policeman said irritably. 'Come on. We'll hae to search elsewhere.'

The dog obeyed, but twice he turned his head to look at the fall. The scent led there, and the scent went on, but he could not make the men understand. He put his

117

nose to the ground again. Paddy Joe had scoured the island and his scent lay everywhere, but nowhere so strong as by the cave entrance.

There was scent coming through the ground. Scent from foxholes, and from under the roots of trees. The dog sniffed, puzzled. He came to a large hole, at the foot of a giant oak, and here the scent poured towards him. He scraped at the ground and barked.

'The dog's out of his heid,' the policeman said.

Far below, Storm heard the bark and answered. He was weak from hunger but his deep bay sounded from the earth and the policeman quieted his own dog and listened.

'The dog's down there,' he said in disbelief.

Tomkin flung himself on the ground, his mouth to the hole, darkening the world completely for Paddy Joe. The trace of light had been a beacon, a consolation, and he was plunged into despair again. He had been dozing and had heard Storm bark but not the sound of the police dog above him.

'Paddy Joe.'

It was a call from the world above, it was a reassurance, and Storm barked joyously, sure that all would be well now that Tomkin was there. Paddy Joe quieted the dog and shouted in his turn.

'I'm down here. In a tunnel. I can't get back.'

There was disbelief on every face. Tomkin stared down at the ground.

'If we dig . . .' he said. His throat was suddenly dry and he felt sick. There was no telling what would happen if they began to dig. The earth might well cave in and bury boy and dog. No knowing how deep they were, no guessing whether the earth covered rock or was loose and friable.

'We'll have you out in no time, Paddy Joe,' Tomkin shouted, but his face was bleak as he spoke and he stood, staring at the two policemen. It was easier to say than to do. They had no idea how to begin.

The police dog and his handler went back to the cottage. Their job was ended. They found the Colonel and Mac about to start on another search and told them the news. Andy came round the corner of the cottage and heard them.

'We don't know how to begin to get the boy out,' the policeman said. 'It sounds as if they're deep in the earth.'

'They're in the old tunnel,' Andy said. 'I hae been looking at the cellar and the door is still there, but it is boarded over. If I could get in . . . I mind the place well. We played there as boys. The tunnels run all through the island and there are branches and caves where the smugglers hid their wares. There's one place where ye crawl through a narrow passage. I could get there . . . the rest of ye are all too big.'

Tomkin had stayed by the foxhole and he called to Paddy Joe. If only he could drop food down the hole. He tried to enlarge it, and earth pattered downwards.

'How deep down are you, Paddy Joe?' he called.

It was impossible to tell. It was like being at the bottom of a narrow well. It was cold and he was glad of the warmth of his dog, curled up close against him as if he knew that Paddy Joe needed heat. Earth trickled past him. It was not going to be possible to dig or send down food. Tomkin knew that but Paddy Joe did not. Hope warmed him, and he was sure it would not be long before he was safe again. He was very hungry.

Mac and Andy and the policeman and the Colonel were back at the old house. They had been joined by several of the villagers, and eager hands shored up the walls round the old cellar, lest they cave in while they were working. The door had been padlocked long ago, to

119

prevent lads wandering in the tunnel systems, as on several occasions village boys had been lost underground. It had not been opened for over fifty years. Andy, filing at the old rusty padlock, wondered briefly if he could find his way. It made him realise he was over seventy now. Time to think of that when he was inside. He knew where the foxhole lay and guessed how he could reach it. And he could make good speed, as he would have a light.

It was over an hour before the door creaked open to reveal the darkness beyond. Tomkin, lying on his coat at the foot of the tree, had heard nothing from Paddy Joe for some time, and hoped the boy was asleep. Paddy Joe was half awake and half dozing. He longed for food. He put his arms round his dog. He wondered if he could ever move again. He was so stiff and his cramped bones ached unbearably.

He heard Tomkin call to say that help was on its way, and slept again, while Andy left the day behind and walked into the long deserted tunnel, his torch blazing in front of him, lighting grey walls and dusty floor and craggy rock that knew no weathering deep under the ground. He shivered. He hated the enclosed dark, the fusty smell and the pressure of earth above him. He would never have come here alone, left to himself, but there was no choice. He was as small as Paddy Joe and no other grown man could crawl under the lowering rock at the end of the passage near the foxhole. The policeman was behind him, but the last part Andy would have to face on his own. His heart raced uncomfortably. Any moment now, he might meet a demon, or a goblin, or worse.

Andy had never been a brave man. Now he was an old man, and he knew many things unguessed by less sensitive folk. Doom lay heavy on the tunnel. There had been hidden deeds down here and at least one man's ghost must haunt the darkness, for he had given the smugglers away and those who were left had taken their revenge and walled him into the tunnel, without food or water, to remember the men he had betrayed. They had intended to rescue him before he died, but fate intervened and the men who immured him went out to fish and the waters took their boat. Long years after, other men found his skeleton and gave him Christian burial in the churchyard on the mainland. If he had stayed to take revenge. It was not a thought to cherish.

The policeman was untroubled by fear of ghosts. He had never explored the place before and was fascinated by the formation, hollowed out over centuries by the passage of the sea and continued in places by man. Here and there tunnels were connected by shafts made by miners. Perhaps they had mined ore. It was difficult to say. Perhaps long ago when history had just begun, little dark men dug into the ground and found some form of wealth. The policeman did not know. His torch lit rough, uneven walls.

Andy, seeing the same walls, felt sudden unreasonable panic. They were scored and cracked and might fall in. It was years since any sort or repair had been done in the shafts, where wooden props were rotting and the air was stale. If it weren't for the boy he would never have set foot here. He remembered that he had a light and Paddy Joe was in the dark and went on, shutting his mind to the fears that clouded it.

They were back in a natural tunnel, where the roof was covered in long growths. Stalactites or stalagmites, the policeman wondered. He had long forgotten the difference.

There was a sudden flurry of wings and the air about them was thick with terror. The light, shining on the bats hanging from the roof, had wakened them. Small bodies swirled, blinded by the torches. Light had never penetrated here before. Andy hated bats. They were worse than owls and he was sure that all of them, in spite of what other people said, were vampires. He threw up his hands to shield his head as a small furry body with a long-eared face darted towards him. The torch dropped on the ground and the light went out. The bulb was broken.

A few hundred yards away, Paddy Joe heard the crash and Storm growled. Paddy Joe had not realised that help would come from underground. He was waiting for digging to begin above him, and he watched the patch of light, hoping it would widen. But dusk was stealing up on day, making long shadows, and the dim patch was fading. Only Tomkin lying above him, now whistling cheerfully, having run out of conversation, was reassurance. It was not easy to talk when every word had to be shouted through several feet of earth, even if there was a hole above him. He suddenly remembered Alice at the bottom of her tunnel and the dormouse and the mock turtle. He would have been surprised to know that Storm was growling because a small mouse had crossed the cave floor, disturbed by Andy's footsteps.

Andy took the remaining torch, leaving the policeman in the dark. He squatted on his haunches, waiting. The policeman was not an imaginative man, and the bats did not trouble him. He could not creep along the little narrow gully into which Andy had just crawled, taking care this time not to drop his light. He had a haversack with him in which was food and a flask of hot coffee, and this he tied to his belt and dragged behind him, easing it over the rough parts which barked his hands and knees. Half-way through the passage he called. No use crippling himself if the lad was not there.

'Paddy Joe!'

Storm barked and Paddy Joe woke and called out.

'I'll be wi' ye in an instant, lad.'

Andy had forgotten his ghosts. The lad was there and would need food and a human voice to cheer him and the dog was alive too and judging by that bark in no bad shape.

There was water in plenty here. Andy had knelt in it and the wet knees of his trousers irritated him. He would pay dearly with the rheumatics for this. It was no game for a man of his age and that over seventy.

But there again he could show the young men a thing or two, and it was no small thing to be rescuing the lad single-handed. Andy's thoughts wavered from one track to another, like an untried pup chasing rabbits, starting new quarry from every bush. It was better than thinking about the ground far above and the things that might hide in the darkness. Andy believed whole-heartedly in the Loch Ness monster and was sure that others of her ilk hid in the caves. If he met one here . . . maybe a ghost would be better. He drew a deep breath. He could stand.

He stretched and shone the torch on Paddy Joe, crouched on the ground. He went over to the boy, forgetting that his torch was dazzling, and he was hidden in the darkness. Paddy Joe stared.

'Who is it?' he said, uncertainly.

Andy turned the torch on his own face.

'I hae food for ye and for the dog,' he said, and brought the flask out of the bag and poured hot coffee. 'Drink it verra slowly, lad. In wee sips now.'

Paddy Joe sipped and felt warmth flood back to his bones. Storm was tearing at a piece of meat, worrying and grumbling, eager to eat. Paddy Joe took a sandwich but found that his hunger had died and he could not face the food. He gnawed at a corner, and left the rest, and Andy put it away again and took off his own coat and put it round Paddy Joe's shoulders.

'Can ye follow me, lad, and we'll make our way back?

They canna dig down to ye. It is too chancy. The earth is loose.'

Paddy Joe did not want to face the tunnel again, nor the narrow passage. But there was no choice and this time there was light. He stood, stiff legs cramped and painful, and Storm sat, watching them closely.

'Come,' said Andy. He called up the foxhole. 'The lad's all right.' Tomkin whistled in answer, and made his way back to the house and the cellar, where a group of men waited, and the Colonel's car and the police car shone their headlights into the gaping dark.

They waited for eternity, each man silent. The Colonel smoked, and Mac took another torch and walked into the passage, followed by Tomkin who could not sit still. He had been into the cottage and put a pan of broth on the fire, and brought blankets with him, and now he needed action. The air in the caves struck cold, and he shivered and wondered how Paddy Joe had fared, and how he had come to be inside the tunnel at all. Presumably Storm had chased down after a fox. If only the lad had not forgotten the dog's training. And there was a rider to that. Tomkin should have insisted. He had been too soft and look where softness led you—to a lost boy and a lost dog and hours of worry, and lucky things were no worse.

Paddy Joe was creeping through the narrow gully. He was thankful for the light that showed the way, but too bemused to look at the cave walls or see the strange growths that hung on every side. Curiosity had died. He wanted food and bed, but he wanted light. He craved for light, needing it desperately, needing sunlight on his face, daylight around him, firelight to warm him. The torchlight was cold as the cave air and in spite of Andy's coat cold had taken total possession of him and his teeth began to chatter. He crept on, and came suddenly into the wider part of the tunnel.

The policeman saw him and reached out a hand, and Paddy Joe cried out. He had not seen the shadow in the darkness. The policeman cursed himself.

'It's all right, lad. Ye're safe. It will only take a few minutes to get ye out of here, and then we will soon hae ye warm and tucked up in bed.'

He was talking to give reassurance. But Paddy Joe was beyond reassurance and his legs refused to obey his head. He flopped to the ground and the big policeman stooped and lifted him. The tunnel was wide enough here. It was only the narrow passage that had stopped anyone but Andy going along.

Storm pattered behind them, anxious to be free of the dark. He walked as close to Paddy Joe as was possible.

Andy left them. He had seen something in the darkness, and as soon as they walked into the light of the headlamps he turned back into the caves. He found the bones. The skeleton of a dog, about the size of a collie. That was one mystery the less and in sudden pity he gathered them together and carried them out into the garden at the end of the cellars, where the ruined walls let in the light. He was a man who loved dogs. His own always received careful burial.

When Paddy Joe was safe and warm in bed with Storm lying on the floor beside him, Andy brought the bones to the cottage.

'The collie dog must have got into the tunnel and died there, and Mistress Campbell did not think to explore the passages,' he said. 'Or she couldn't get through the gully.'

Tomkin left the lamp burning in Paddy Joe's bedroom and waited beside the bed until the boy was asleep. He went into the garden and looked at the bones and thought, with a sudden pang, 'There but for the Grace of God went the boy and the dog today.'

The four men dug the collie's grave, in the woods

where once he had roamed, and as Andy threw in the last shovel of earth he thought he saw a woman standing under the trees. She held out her hands to him in supplication. Tomkin put a stone above the little grave. They would inscribe it later, and seek through the diaries to find an apt quotation. Andy turned his head again. The woman had gone. Moonlight shone through the close grown trees and the island was peaceful.

No more ghosts would sorrow the place.

It was a week before Paddy Joe was fit again. He had suffered in the boat. He had suffered underground. He was bruised and sore and stiff and ached all over. Feverish dreams racked him, and Tomkin's anger died and was spent in anxiety. He rarely left Paddy Joe's bedside. But at last the boy was well. Another day and he could get up.

Tomorrow, thought the Colonel, he would catch the biggest fish he had ever seen. He would take the boy with him. They had left Paddy Joe too much alone. It was hard, after years without a boy about the place, to remember how boys felt. Tomorrow, thought Tomkin, he would make sure the boy trained the dog.

Paddy Joe lying in bed, recovered from his ordeal, was thinking too. Tomorrow he would train Storm properly. And he would try to remember to think in future before he acted. Tomkin had been angry, when Paddy Joe was well enough to chide.

'It's your own fault, Paddy Joe,' he'd said. 'Think on. Nobody made you go out alone. Nobody made you take the boat and nearly drown. And what was worse, you put others in danger. Men with families who had to take the lifeboat and rescue you. They could easily have died. And Andy had to crawl down the tunnel and rescue you, too. He's an old man, Paddy Joe. And a good job he is, too. None of the younger men knew about the caves. They were sealed up years ago. You don't know how lucky you were. You'd no right to run off. Grow up, and think.'

Paddy Joe had had hours to think. The trouble was that it wasn't always easy to remember, but at least he'd try. He reached out his hand. The dog was warm and solid and reassuring, alive and breathing, on the floor beside the bed.

Storm looked up. Paddy Joe patted his dog and the Alsatian licked his hand. Moonlight barred the bed, and an owl flew across the windy sky. As the Colonel walked indoors from the garden a leaf blew against his coat. He picked it up and turned it over, and looked at Tomkin.

'It's never too late,' he said.

He put the leaf on the table. It would remind them in the morning. The house slept, and the wind roved among the trees. Outside the window the wild beasts lived their own lives, ignorant of man. Tomorrow would be a new beginning. The leaf blew off the table, and the wind mocked the night.

THE END

If you would like to receive a newsletter telling you about our new children's books, fill in the coupon with your name and address and send it to:

Gillian Osband,

Transworld Publishers Ltd,

Century House,

61–63 Uxbridge Road, Ealing,

London, W5 5SA

Name ....

Address ....

....

CHILDREN'S NEWSLETTER

All the books on the previous pages are available at your bookshop or can be ordered direct from Transworld Publishers Ltd., Cash Sales Dept. P.O. Box 11, Falmouth, Cornwall.

Please send full name and address together with cheque or postal order—no currency, and allow 45p per book to cover postage and packing (plus 20p each for additional copies).